"Break! He's on your six," the Executioner warned

When the Harrier flashed in front of the canopy, the Russian pressed the cannon trigger, sending twenty high-explosive-tipped shells after the wildly skidding jet.

The shell that smashed into the turbine compressor of the Harrier's Rolls-Royce engine shredded the spinning turbine blades into red-hot shrapnel. In an instant the guts of the jet were useless.

Jack Grimaldi didn't even have time to shout a warning as the intrument panel went crazy. Instead, he slammed his back against the armored seat and jerked hard on the ejection-sequence handle.

The rear seat fired first, blowing an unsuspecting Mack Bolan through the top of the closed canopy. A second later, Grimaldi's seat fired, too, and both men were clear of the doomed Harrier. Their automatic releases functioned to separate them from their seats and popped their parachute canopies open above them.

Freed from Grimaldi's hands on the controls, the Harrier flipped onto its back and started to come apart in the air as it went into an inverted flat spin. An explosion in the engine bay sent burning debris showering into the jungle.

The Executioner and the Stony Man pilot were dropping into enemy territory without food, water, ammo or weapons....

MACK BOLAN ®

The Executioner

DON PENDLETON'S
THE EXECUTIONER®
SHOOT DOWN

A GOLD EAGLE BOOK FROM
WORLDWIDE®

TORONTO • NEW YORK • LONDON
AMSTERDAM • PARIS • SYDNEY • HAMBURG
STOCKHOLM • ATHENS • TOKYO • MILAN
MADRID • WARSAW • BUDAPEST • AUCKLAND

First edition June 1995
ISBN 0-373-61198-6

Special thanks and acknowledgment to
Michael Kasner for his contribution to this work.

SHOOT DOWN

Printed in U.S.A.

If we believe a thing to be bad, and if we have a right to prevent it, it is our duty to try to prevent it, and to damn the consequences.

> —Lord Milner,
> Speech, Glasgow,
> November 26, 1909

No amount of covert action against the narcobarons can compensate for the lives lost to the drug trade. But it is my duty to forge on, doing what I must, one mission at a time, to end this terrible scourge.

> —Mack Bolan

To the ceaseless efforts of the men and women of the DEA.
God keep.

PROLOGUE

Over the Golden Triangle

United States Air Force Major James Boyd was bored out of his mind as he piloted his E-3 Sentry aerial-surveillance aircraft through the sky above Southeast Asia where Burma, Thailand and Laos come together. This mountainous region of dense jungle and inhospitable tribesmen was infamously known as the Golden Triangle, the place where the majority of the world's heroin supply originated.

To make the drug, the mountain tribes of the region grew opium poppies and carefully gathered the sap from the mature seed pods. The sap was dried in the sun, then processed in jungle laboratories into raw opium. The opium was further refined into high-grade heroin and fed into the world's underground drug pipeline. Weeks later it reappeared on the streets and in the back alleys of the world's cities, spreading death and destruction to thousands.

In the United States, heroin use had declined during the cocaine boom of the eighties. But now China White was back, and it was back in a big way. With this new demand had come increased opium poppy production. The Golden Triangle was producing more than seventy percent of the world's heroin supply, well over a thousand tons a year.

Jim Boyd was bored because he was flying surveillance missions for the American Drug Enforcement Administration. The major, his four engined surveillance plane and its crew had been lent to the drug agency in an attempt to stem the never-ending flow of heroin. This time, though, the DEA was trying to stop the illicit drug at its source rather than waiting for it to reach the United States.

The sophisticated sensor equipment on the E-3 Sentry was meant to penetrate the triple-canopy jungle and spot the refining labs and storage areas believed to be hiding below. When these operations were discovered and mapped, the DEA hoped to convince the Thai and Burmese governments to move against them.

But as far as Boyd was concerned, the DEA guys were weenies who played stupid games with drug lords instead of doing what was necessary to put an end to the drug trade once and for all. He felt that they didn't because of politics. It couldn't be all that difficult to find these guys and put them out of business permanently. There were still enough B-52 bombers left in the inventory to put together an Arc Light force as they had done during the Vietnam and Gulf wars. A week of around-the-clock bombing should take care of them. And if they tried to get back into business, they could always be bombed again.

Screwing around in the air the way he was doing, was a complete waste of a good airplane and a top-notch crew, to say nothing of his personal time. But it all counted toward twenty, and he had only two more short years before he could finally hang up his blue suit and start that charter service in the Bahamas he dreamed about.

"We've got a fighter inbound, Major." The radarman's voice on the intercom broke the pilot's thoughts of small white seaplanes landing on crystal-clear bays next to verdant Caribbean islands.

"Is it squawking IFF?" the pilot asked. The drug surveillance flights were being coordinated with both the Thai and Burmese authorities so there shouldn't be any problem with their air forces.

"That's a big negative, sir," the radar operator answered. "He's not transmitting anything on any channel. No IFF and no flight number."

Suddenly Major Jim Boyd wasn't bored. They were close enough to the Chinese border that a MiG pilot could have strayed across the invisible boundary to see who they were and what they were doing so close to his country. Dealing with those guys was always dicey, so he'd better get on the horn fast and see what the flyer's problem was.

He switched his VHF radio over to Guard Channel, the international emergency frequency, and pressed the talk button. "Unknown fighter bearing two-two-six, this is United States Drug Enforcement Flight 38 Alpha out of Nakhon Phanom, Thailand. Come in, please."

When he released his microphone button, all he heard was static. English was the international aviation language, so the pilot should have understood him. He tried again. "Unknown fighter bearing—"

"He's painting us!" The radar operator's voice was shrill as he announced that the fighter's targeting radar was looking at them.

Boyd's head snapped around to see if he could spot the intruder, but the sky was empty behind him.

"He's got lock-on!" the radar operator screamed. "Fuck! He's launched!"

"Mayday! Mayday!" Boyd's voice rose as he pushed the nose of his big plane into a dive. "This is DEA 38 Alpha. We're under attack by an unknown fighter over the Golden Triangle. Mayday! Mayday! If anyone's up here, we need help! Mayday! May—"

Ex-Russian air force Captain Yuri Galan grimaced when he opened the canopy of his Yak-141B jump jet and was assailed by the damp heat and stench of decay that was so much a part of this tropical rain forest. He had been living in this stinking jungle for almost two months now but still wasn't used to the heat and humidity, to say nothing of the smell. But, for the amount of money he was being paid to be an aerial mercenary for these people, he would endure it even if it killed him.

Other of his old Red air force comrades were also making a little on the side, renting out their jet fighters by the mission to the many ethnic armies fighting in the breakaway republics. He had made many such flights himself for government forces in the Georgian Republic's civil war. The job had paid fairly well, even

with his having to give a cut to the mechanics, the ordnance men and his squadron commander, but it hadn't
been nearly enough. Not when his targets started
shooting back at him with increasing accuracy.

When he had returned from a ground-attack mission in Georgia with his Su-22 riddled with 23 mm
holes and the jet engine threatening to blow up at any
minute, he decided to find other employment. Prefer-
ably employment where people didn't shoot back at
him.

His new contract as a flying mercenary for the drug
lords of the Golden Triangle was much more to his
liking. He was drawing ten thousand dollars U.S. a
month, plus a five-thousand-dollar bonus each time he
made a heroin delivery. The way he figured it, after a
little more than a year here he could retire back in
Moscow and live the life of a millionaire. At least a
Russian-ruble millionaire.

He owed it all to the sleek jet fighter that the drug
lord's troops were pushing back under the trees, and to
the quirk of fate that had put him in the right place at
the right time.

A month after his last mission as a mercenary for the
Georgians, he had been transferred to the Zhukovsky
flight test center some forty miles outside of Moscow.
It had cost him quite a bit of his hoarded mercenary's
wages to get the plum assignment, but it had paid off
in a way he never expected when he had been assigned
to the Yak-141 VSTOL fighter test program.

The Yak-141 had been designed as the old Soviet air
forces's answer to the threat posed by NATO's Har-

rier jump jet. The advent of the British-designed Harrier in the NATO inventory had caught the Russians at a serious disadvantage in battlefield tactical aviation. They, too, had played around with various vertical-takeoff jet-fighter designs back in the sixties while the British were developing the Harrier. The Soviet attempts hadn't been very successful, however, and they were abandoned on the premise that the British designers would run into the same engineering brick wall and abandon the idea, as well.

Then, against all odds the Harrier had been perfected and the Russians found themselves desperately playing catch-up. The Harrier's outstanding performance as a ground-attack fighter in the short but furious Falkland Islands War only added to the desperation.

The Yakovlev design bureau's first response to the Harrier threat was a VSTOL fighter designated the Yak-38, NATO-code-named Forger. It was a blatant rip-off of the Harrier's twin-vectored thrust-nozzle system at the rear of the fuselage combined with a purely Russian lift-jet system in the middle.

The problem with the Yak-38 was that while it was more or less as good as a Harrier, it was no better. It could make a vertical takeoff and landing like a Harrier and it was a bit faster, being supersonic in clean configuration without underwing ordnance. But it didn't have the lift capability of its NATO counterpart, was short ranged and wasn't a good ground-attack fighter. It ended up being used as Russia's first naval-air-force-carrier jet fighter.

Back at their drawing boards, the Yakovlev design team tried harder and came up with the Yak-141, code-named Free-style. This was to be the jump jet for the twenty-first century. To start with, it was fully super-sonic. Secondly, it could carry a full ordnance load and had sufficient range to be a devastating attack fighter. It was also a superb air-to-air dogfighter, capable of taking on any front-line fighter in the world and beat-ing it.

The Yak-141 was the best VSTOL fighter prototype in the world, surpassing even the Harrier II, which was just coming into service with NATO and American forces. But in the new Russia of the nineties, there was no money to pay for its continued development into a service-qualified fighter.

Yakovlev pressed on, however, spending precious private-company money on the design until the sec-ond prototype crashed during a bad-weather test land-ing on a Russian aircraft carrier. The single surviving prototype was parked, and the program seemed doomed.

But while the Russian military wasn't buying new hardware, the Russian aircraft industry wasn't quite ready to throw in the towel and start manufacturing household appliances. Russian aircraft were among the best in the world, and there was no reason why they couldn't find a niche in the world's booming arms market. This was certainly the attitude of the engi-neers of the Yakovlev design bureau.

In an attempt to attract foreign interest in their products, the surviving Yak-141 prototype was dusted off, repainted and sent to the '93 Farnborough International Airshow in England. Yuri Galan went on the trip with the factory team as the plane's backup pilot.

After the first demonstration flight at Farnborough, two Hong Kong businessmen contacted Yakovlev with a proposition. They said they represented a client who wished to purchase a Yak-141 and a full set of spares and ground-support equipment. The amount offered for the jump jet almost sent the Yakovlev representatives into cardiac arrest. Yakovlev desperately needed a hard-currency infusion to continue work on the VSTOL design, which they saw as their firm's salvation. And Kuhn Sa, the lord of the Golden Triangle, needed a very special jet fighter that could defend his empire from aerial snoops.

So it was that a Russian aircraft manufacturer and an Asian drug lord came to an arrangement. But rather than sell them the aircraft, Yakovlev offered an improved version, a third prototype just now being completed at the factory, for the same price. Built as a private venture with company funds, the third Yak-141 wasn't even on the government's books, so no one would notice if it turned up missing. As an improved version of the initial prototype, the design bureau had designated it the Yak-141B. When it had been picked up on U.S. spy satellites, it was code-named Freehand to distinguish it from the earlier Yak-141s.

As for Galan's part in the deal, he signed on as the jump jet's mercenary pilot. Money from his new employer speeded his resignation from the Russian air force, and he was taken on at Yakovlev as a "foreign sales representative."

GENERAL KUHN SA was waiting to meet Yuri Galan.

The Russian pilot had never heard of Kuhn Sa, or the Golden Triangle for that matter, prior to being contacted by the Hong Kong businessmen in England. Although he had just delivered his Yak-141B to the drug lord, he still didn't know a lot about the man except that he was his new employer and he paid well.

Stepping down from the jet, Galan turned to face the one man in the welcoming delegation who wasn't openly displaying a weapon. Snapping to attention, he rendered a crisp salute, military-academy style. "Captain Yuri Galan reporting, sir."

The man returned his salute and spoke in what sounded like Chinese. "The general welcomes you," an aide at his side translated into Russian. "And he is happy to see your amazing airplane."

Kuhn Sa was a small, wiry, unimpressive-looking man, but Galan saw great strength in his flint black eyes. Though his name had never appeared on the Fortune 500 list, that strength had made him one of the world's wealthiest men. And his great wealth came from the beautiful poppies that grew so prolifically in the fields beyond the jungle.

The six bodyguards accompanying the general looked like tough fighting men. Their uniforms and weapons were worn but immaculate, and their hard eyes never left the Russian pilot during the entire interview.

"You will make your first delivery tomorrow night," the general said after the introductions and small talk were out of the way. "I am told that your airplane can carry a metric-ton load for almost a thousand miles."

"That is only a one-way trip, General," Galan answered respectfully. "If I am to make the return trip from that distance, I would have to be able to refuel."

"I will have fuel waiting there for you. Good fuel."

Clean fuel and a place big enough to land were all any pilot needed to conduct business. And since the Yak could land any place a helicopter could, the fuel was the most important of the two.

"There will be no problem, then," Galan stated.

When the general left, the Russian-speaking aide remained behind. "I am Major Yu Lim. I will be the voice of the general and your—how do you say it?— operations officer."

Galan stiffened to attention as he would have to a Russian air force major. "At your command, Major."

Lim's face remained expressionless. "I will show you to your quarters now."

Lim led Galan to a small bamboo house set well back under the towering trees. Two young women in tribal dress were standing by the door with their hands clasped in front of them and their heads bowed.

"They will see to your needs," Lim explained curtly. "I have taught them enough Russian that you should be able to get by."

With that, Lim turned and left Galan to his new life in the Golden Triangle.

IN THE MONTH AND A HALF since his arrival, Galan had made one drug delivery a week. Six tons of heroin had been flown to places as far apart as China and Afghanistan.

Being a Russian, the pilot had no experience with drugs or drug addicts. Nor did he care that some of the heroin he ferried was destined for the back alleys and subway stations of his Mother Russia. He had been away from Moscow for a long time and hadn't run into any of the growing army of drug addicts in the new Russia. Even if he had, though, he would have had no pity for them. As far as he was concerned, anyone who took drugs was weak and deserved the untimely death that would surely come.

Beyond making the drug deliveries, there had been little for the Russian to do except service his fighter, eat and sleep. He had ventured into the jungle around the hidden camp only once. He had gone less than two hundred meters down a well-used trail before encountering a large snake. Since then he had stayed close to the small camp.

The general had recruited a team of mercenary Chinese jet mechanics under the command of a sergeant crew chief who did most of the work on the Yak. Sergeant Chow was a capable man who spoke passable Russian, although with a strong accent. He was well trained on Russian-designed jet engines and fire-control systems, so there was little for Galan to do himself, which was just as well. He was a pilot, not a black-shirt mechanic.

The feminine companionship the general had so thoughtfully provided helped Galan while away the long hours, both by day and by night. The women were charming and exotic to his eyes and were certainly as good at what they did as he was at flying his Yak fighter. On top of that, they were good cooks and were learning Russian quickly.

The general had also been thoughtful enough to see that his pilot had a supply of Russian vodka, and it was Stolichnaya, the high-test export liquor, rather than the rotgut he drank at home.

All in all, it was as good a life as could be expected in the middle of a jungle. Then had come word from the general about the American DEA surveillance plane.

Since his initial meeting on the day he arrived, Galan hadn't seen Kuhn Sa again. Major Lim acted as liaison officer and passed on mission orders. Beyond that, Lim wasn't around much, either, which was okay with Galan. There was something about the Chinese officer's flat, expressionless eyes and harsh features that bothered him in a way he couldn't explain.

One evening Galan looked up from his dinner to see Major Lim approaching his bamboo house. Frowning, Galan hoped that he could finish his meal before he had to go somewhere. It had taken the Russian a couple of weeks to get accustomed to the spicy cuisine of the Southeast Asian highlands, but it had grown on him. Now he looked forward to every meal.

"There is a small problem the general wants you to take care of for him," Major Lim said after one of Galan's women served him tea.

"And that is?"

"The American Drug Enforcement Administration has flown a surveillance plane into Thailand, and they plan to use it to spy on our operation here."

"What does the general want me to do about it?"

"He wants you to shoot the plane down."

"An American plane?"

"It is a spy plane. It threatens both our operation here and your health, should it discover that you and your fighter are flying out of here."

That was a good enough argument for Galan. His value to Kuhn Sa was tied to his fighter. Without it he was worth nothing to the operation. So if he had to shoot down an American plane to protect the Yak, he would.

Before he could do that, however, he had to arm his fighter. Even though the Yak had been a development aircraft, it had been fitted with an internal 30 mm GS-301 cannon in the belly and had a "look down-shoot down" fire-control system borrowed from a MiG-29. It also had two "hot shoe" weapons pylons mounted under each wing. What Galan didn't have, though, were missiles to hang on the pylons or ammunition for the cannon. To save weight, the Yak had been completely unarmed on the initial flight south.

"Tell the general that I will need ammunition and missiles if I am to do this."

Lim handed him a ballpoint pen and a notepad. "Write down the Russian designation for the ammunition you need, and it will be delivered."

Though he had doubts, Galan did as Lim asked and handed back the notepad. "If he can get this for me, it will be no problem."

Lim put the notepad unread into his pocket. "He will get it."

TO THE RUSSIAN'S SURPRISE, a Chinese-army-marked Mil-8 helicopter brought a load of 30 mm ammunition and Chinese copies of the Russian AA-2 Atoll missile into the clearing early the next day. The general might be living in the middle of a jungle, but obviously his tentacles had a far reach. He had wanted weapons to arm his hired fighter, and they had appeared like magic.

The Chinese crew chief grinned broadly when he saw the Chinese characters on the sides of the crates. "These missiles work good on Yankee air pirates," he told Galan.

"Let's get them mounted," the pilot ordered.

Sergeant Chow shouted a string of rapid-fire Chinese, and the ground crew went to work uncrating the missiles.

Since the Chinese heat-seeking, air-to-air missiles were copies of the Russian AA-2 Atoll, they hooked up to the Yak's weapons pylons with no difficulty. The Chinese might not be able to design their own weapons, but they made good copies of other nations' designs. Starting back in the days of the Korean War, they produced both Russian and American weapons for their own use and for sale on the world market. Along the way they had made minor changes or improvements to some of them, particularly to the aircraft. But these Russian air-to-air missiles were exact transistor-for-transistor copies of the originals. They would have no trouble mating up with the jet's fire-control and targeting systems.

While the ground crew mounted the missiles, Galan personally supervised the loading of the 30 mm ammunition into the ammo bay in the jet's belly. When Sergeant Chow's men were finished, he double-checked the firing connections for the missiles on the pylons.

"You ready now for sure, Captain." Chow grinned proudly.

"I hope so."

Once the Yak was armed, Galan had to wait until Kuhn Sa got word that the American spy plane was on its way. When Lim brought the word, Galan was in the cockpit and on his way in under five minutes.

The mission itself went like a training exercise in a flight simulator.

Galan's radar picked up the four-engined spy plane eighty kilometers away. He went directly into an intercept course, lined up on the big jet from the stern, got a lock-on and fired a single heat-seeking missile from nine kilometers out. The Atoll hit the left inboard engine and detonated in a ball of flame.

The explosion tore off the wing, and the surveillance plane did a slow roll to the left as it plunged toward the jungle.

Galan followed the doomed aircraft down until it impacted in the jungle and disappeared in a billowing fireball. After mapping the location of the burning wreckage, he banked his Yak to the north.

On the flight back he didn't waste any thought on the crew of the downed American surveillance plane. To him it had just been a job. He flew a jet fighter, and jet fighters were designed to shoot down other planes and kill people.

Plus this wasn't the first plane he had downed. Two Georgian helicopters had fallen prey to the guns and missiles of his Sukhoi fighter during his mercenary missions over the breakaway republic. The only difference this time was that the plane had been American.

MAJOR LIM WAS WAITING when Galan landed back at the clearing. The thin man smiled for a change as he approached the pilot. "The general has authorized me to give you a large bonus for destroying the American spy plane. It will be added to your Hong Kong account."

Galan knew that most of the credit belonged to the sleek VSTOL fighter being pushed back under the towering triple-canopy jungle, but the money was nice and that's why he was flying the Yak. "Thank him for me."

As soon as Lim walked away, Sergeant Chow appeared. Galan had noticed that the easygoing Chinese sergeant didn't like to be around Lim, either.

"It worked just like you said it would," he told the crew chief.

Chow just smiled.

1

"And that's all we have," Barbara Price said as she switched off the reel-to-reel tape recorder. Air Force Major Jim Boyd's last panicked "Mayday" seemed to hang in the air of the War Room in the basement of the Stony Man farmhouse. "The E-3's radio quit transmitting right after that."

Though Stony Man Farm was in Virginia's lovely Shenandoah Valley, for a brief moment the air seemed to carry a trace of the heat and humidity of the tropics. Once more Southeast Asia had claimed American lives, but this time it had been in the war against drugs, not communism.

"Have they found the wreckage yet?" Mack Bolan asked.

Once Stony Man's chief operative, the big man now maintained a loose association with the Farm, while free to choose and carry out his own missions.

"No," Price replied, shaking her head. Tall, slender and honey blond, she still looked like the fashion model she had been during college. In her washed-out, form-fitting blue jeans, cowboy boots and open-collar shirt, she looked nothing like what she was, the mission controller for the nation's most top-secret strike force, the Stony Man Sensitive Operations Group.

"And that's not the worst part, Striker," the man seated at the far end of the table stated.

Hal Brognola was also a big man, but he had more bulk around his middle from commanding a desk in the Justice Department in Washington instead of working the streets as he had done in his younger years. He drew his paycheck from the Justice Department, but his orders came directly from the Oval Office. His job was to direct the covert operations of SOG as the President's personal representative.

The Executioner turned in his chair to face Brognola. "What do you mean?"

"Since the E-3 Sentry was shot down, four other planes searching for the wreckage have been lost in the same area. One was another DEA ship, and the rest of them were Thai air force. One of the Thai pilots managed to get off a short radio message about being attacked by a jet fighter, but that's all we know."

Bolan frowned. "Do you think the drug lords have an air force now?"

"It appears to be a real possibility," Brognola stated flatly.

"Why was the DEA overflying that area? I didn't know we were doing that."

"Heroin exports from Southeast Asia have climbed to record levels recently," the big Fed explained. "Our intelligence indicates that the Golden Triangle poppy production is up some twenty-five percent. The worst thing is that a greater percentage of it is getting through. And rather than shipping it as raw opium, it's coming out of there as refined China White. This means that there are some new labs in the jungle. The DEA figured that if they could identify some of these new facilities, they could pressure the local governments to move against them.

"You didn't hear about the flights because the DEA was trying to keep them ultralow-profile," Brognola went on. "They borrowed the plane from the Air Force and based it out of the Thai air base at Nakhon Phanom. Obviously they weren't keeping it low-profile enough."

"What does the Man want us to do about this that the DEA can't?"

"First off—" Brognola leaned forward in his chair "—the President wants the wreckage of that surveillance plane found and the bodies recovered. You know how he is about bringing our men home. With the Vietnam MIA issue in the news again, he doesn't want to add more names to the list."

Bolan nodded. While recovering the bodies of the dead wasn't a combat priority for him, bringing them home for burial when it was all over was entirely another matter. Every man, no matter how he had died, deserved to spend his final rest in his native soil.

"Then," the big Fed continued, "he wants us to find that jet fighter and put it out of business. Sitting back and allowing those people to get away with something like this sets a bad precedent."

The Executioner could only agree. If the Asian and Latin American drug cartels ever decided to branch out into full-scale military activities, the body count in the war against drugs would skyrocket. So far, the main reason they hadn't done this was the threat of international military retaliation. Only recognized nations were allowed to have organized armies and air forces. If the drug lords of the Golden Triangle were building an air force, it had to be shut down immediately.

But the same international laws that frowned on free-lance military forces also frowned on the United States using its legitimate military strength to wipe out traffickers. Once more, Stony Man would attempt to do what could more easily be done by the military if politicians had the courage to let them do it.

"And of course," Brognola added unnecessarily, "he wants to keep this as quiet as possible, which is why he has turned it over to us. Our relations with the Thais aren't good right now. The DEA implicated a powerful cabinet minister in a smuggling payoff recently, and it's caused waves. Our ambassador was almost recalled over it."

"What's the plan?" Bolan asked.

The justice man opened the red-banded manila folder in front of him. "The Marine Corps is lending us one of their two-seat Harrier II TAV-8B jump jets to conduct the search for the wreckage. You'll be using it instead of a chopper in case that jet fighter shows up."

"Jack's driving?" Bolan asked. Jack Grimaldi was Stony Man's ace pilot. If this mystery jet fighter came up to challenge them, Grimaldi would deal with it.

Brognola nodded.

Price glanced up at the twenty-four-hour clock on the wall over the large-scale world map. "As a matter of fact, Jack's due in right about now."

Bolan pushed his chair back. "I'll go meet him."

JACK GRIMALDI GRINNED when he saw his old friend Mack Bolan waiting for him at the edge of the helipad. The two of them went back a long way. If the Executioner was at Stony Man, it meant that they were about to go on another mission together.

Feeding in a little rudder pedal on the Bell Jet-Ranger he had flown from Washington, D.C., Grimaldi dropped the collective to kill the lift to the rotors and touched the skids down. He almost brushed Bolan with the tips of the blades, but the big man hadn't moved an inch. He knew that Jack could land that chopper on the head of a pin if he had to.

The pilot killed the fuel to the turbine, grabbed his flight bag and, stepping down, got right to the point. "What's the deal this time?"

"You're going to love this one, Jack. You get to play with a Marine Harrier jump jet."

"Where're we going?"

"The Golden Triangle. Someone's been shooting down everything that flies over it. The man wants it found ASAP and taken out."

"Sounds like fun."

Over the years Bolan had heard the Golden Triangle called many things, but *fun* wasn't one of the words people usually used. Only Grimaldi would say that venturing into that deep green graveyard of men could be fun.

"What's our opposition this time?" the pilot asked.

"That's what we're going there to find out."

"When do we leave?"

"Can I have a second cup of coffee first?"

"Only if you put a hustle on it." Grimaldi smiled broadly. "I want to get my hands on that Harrier."

IN THE WAR ROOM of the farmhouse, Aaron Kurtzman had wheeled his chair in to join Barbara Price and Hal Brognola for the second half of the briefing. The Stony Man computer expert knew that precious little had been discovered about the Golden Triangle in the electronic world. Recon satellite passes over the area had shown nothing except triple-canopy jungle. All they had to go on was the general location of the missing plane's last radio transmission. That didn't mean that Kurtzman had given up, however. He would continue monitoring the region day and night until the mission was over.

When Bolan returned with Grimaldi, Kurtzman quickly ran over the basics again for the pilot's benefit. He flashed a map of the area where Burma, Thailand and Laos come together—the Golden Triangle—on the big-screen monitor. With a few quick keystrokes, he blocked out an area almost directly in the center of it.

"As near as I can tell, that's where the DEA plane went down," he said. "The Thai jet that got off the transmission about the enemy fighter didn't file a flight plan, so we don't know where he was when he was attacked.''

More keystrokes put a grid over the blocked-out area. ''When you get there, you'll start by flying a preprogrammed search pattern until you've covered every square mile of the entire area.''

''What if we dry-hole?'' Grimaldi asked.

''Fly the pattern again,'' Brognola broke in. ''The President is serious about recovering those people.''

''Got it.''

When Kurtzman had gone over the details, Brognola slid two red-bordered packets across the table to Bolan and Grimaldi. ''Your contact in Thailand is Jim Ransom, the Bangkok DEA station chief. He's an old Asian hand and has been working on this since we noticed the increase in opium production. All he knows about you two is that you're special agents who have been sent out from the head office to take over the aerial-search end of it.''

He glanced down at the packet. ''Your IDs are in there, as well as all the paperwork you'll need to keep up your cover. You're leaving this afternoon.''

2

Bangkok, Thailand

DEA station chief Jim Ransom frowned as he read the fax that had just come in over the wire. Ransom was a heavyset man, showing every one of his forty-six years. He wore his hair cut military short to try to hide the fact that he was losing it, but it wasn't working. He just looked like a balding man with a bad haircut.

Ransom was an old hand at drug enforcement, but that didn't mean he was as secure as he would have liked to be at that point in his career. He was under tremendous pressure from Washington about his office's lack of progress in combating the increased heroin shipments coming out of Thailand.

The loss of the surveillance plane had made a bad situation worse. And the fact that he hadn't been able to make any headway finding it wasn't helping matters. Now that the Thai government had lost some of its own planes looking for it, they were calling off their search, as well, which the Justice Department wasn't going to like. He was in an unenviable position.

Ransom stared blankly at the fax in his hand. This latest twist wasn't going to help him, either, and might well be the beginning of the end for him.

"What's wrong, Jim?" The young man standing by the window overlooking the crowded street below correctly read the expression on Ransom's face.

Brad Winston was newly transferred into the Bangkok field office, and he saw the assignment as his chance to make his mark in the DEA. Even so, he considered the Bangkok station a hellhole and intended to move on as soon as he possibly could. His biggest problem was that his boss was proving to be of little use to a man who wanted to be on the fast track to the top. So far, he had been able to keep his contempt for Ransom hidden, but just barely.

As far as Winston was concerned, the older man was a perfect example of why the DEA hadn't been able to put an end to the blatant drug trafficking in Thailand. Passive measures like surveillance flights were all fine and good to lay groundwork. But stronger action was needed to send a message to the drug lords of the Golden Triangle.

Ransom's eyes were tired when he looked over at his assistant. "Washington's sending a couple of trouble-shooters in tomorrow to take over the search for the downed plane. They're concerned because I haven't been able to recover the bodies yet."

"Who are these guys?"

"Someone named Mike Belasko and a pilot named Jack Grimaldi."

"You ever heard of them?"

"No," Ransom replied. "But there's so many new guys back in the States now that I really don't know anyone anymore."

And that's why Ransom was stuck in this miserable hellhole, Winston thought. He didn't know how to network. If there was anything he was learning from his boss, it was not to get out of touch with the people who really mattered to an agent's career. And all of those people were in the U.S., not places like Bangkok.

Even so, he had to admit that Thailand was where the action was. He had the Georgetown credentials, true, but for his career to follow the right path, he had to see some action fast. Fortunately Ransom's preoccupation with the missing surveillance plane was giving him a chance to show what he could do under fire. The DEA liked high-profile busts, interdictions as they called them, and he had a big one on the burner.

The last thing Winston needed was for a couple of hotshots from the States to come in and steal his thunder. To prevent that from happening, he had to get his show on the road fast. And to do that, he needed Ransom to sign off on his proposal.

"Don't worry about them," he told his boss. "We've got a firm grip on the situation, and we can handle it ourselves. We should be hearing from the ground-search team before too much longer."

"I don't know if the Thais are really sending their people up there. I've got a gut feeling that they're sandbagging us again."

Winston had to get his boss's mind off that downed plane. As far as he was concerned, the dead could rot in the jungle. Bringing them out wouldn't do anything to help him. "Have you given any more thought to that joint-interdiction operation I brought you?"

To help grease the skids, Winston had presented his plan to Ransom as having been cooked up by the Thai special-forces officer he was working with. He had told Major Phem, however, that the plan had originated from the DEA headquarters in Arlington, Virginia. Since the two men had never met, it was unlikely that his maneuvering would ever be found out.

"You say that the Thais have signed off on it?" Ransom asked.

Winston nodded. "They're just waiting for us to give them the go-ahead," he lied.

"I guess we'd better get on board, then," Ransom said wearily. "That last thing I need right now is a complaint from them that we're not playing ball."

Winston was barely able to contain himself. "I'll get right on it, Jim. Major Phem is champing at the bit to get going."

"I hope he's got his shit together on this. I've got to meet those two guys at Nakhon Phanom tomorrow and I don't need any more fuckups."

"Don't worry," Winston promised. "This thing'll go like clockwork."

"It had better."

THE THAI AIR FORCE BASE at Nakhon Phanom had once been a major staging point for the American air war against the North Vietnamese and the Ho Chi Minh Trail. During the long war years, the roar of both jet and piston aircraft engines had sounded across the tarmac twenty-four hours a day, seven days a week.

Since the end of the war, though, air traffic at Naked Fanny, as the American fliers had called it, was a mere trickle compared to what it had been back in the glory days. Though most of the extensive facilities the Americans had built during the war were not now in use, they were still intact. A few were currently being used by the Thai air force units stationed at the base, and the DEA contracted with them for a hangar, operations shack and ground support for their own aircraft.

For Bolan and Grimaldi's clandestine mission, a solitary hangar at the far end of the airfield had been reactivated. The Marine Harrier II had arrived the day before with a ten-man ground-support team and a twenty-man security force under the command of a Marine aviation captain and a gunnery sergeant. Their job was to service the jet and keep it as far from prying eyes as possible.

Grimaldi and Bolan had flown directly from Bangkok to the air force base, and the first thing the pilot wanted to do was check in on their ride. When they parked their borrowed DEA Jeep in front of the closed hangar doors, two hard-eyed Marine sentries in camouflage utilities, steel helmets and flak vests stepped out to challenge them.

"Mike Belasko and Jack Grimaldi," Bolan announced as he pulled out the DEA identification card the Stony Man team had provided for this mission. Grimaldi did the same, and the Marine corporal carefully examined the photos on both cards before silently waving the men through.

"What do they think this is, the Manhattan Project?" Grimaldi asked when he spotted the sandbagged machine-gun bunker off to the side, manned by two more Marine guards.

"They're just making sure we have the place to ourselves. You know what happened to the last bunch of guys who flew out of here."

A young Marine captain wearing gold wings on his flight suit was supervising the crew swarming over the Harrier. More specifically he was watching an aircraft mechanic who was working inside the open nose cone of the jet.

"If you lay that wrench on the radar dish again, Williams," the captain said evenly, "I swear that I'm going to stuff it up your nose. After, of course, I've assigned you to permanent latrine-cleaning duty for the rest of your enlistment. Is that understood?"

The mechanic stiffened and clutched the offending wrench even tighter. "Aye, aye, sir."

"Good."

The Marine pilot turned to watch Bolan and Grimaldi approach. "Are you the two DEA guys who're supposed to fly this thing?" He jerked his thumb back toward the Harrier.

"I'm the pilot. Jack Grimaldi, DEA. Mike Belasko, here, is the special agent in charge."

"I'm Captain Dave Jenson." The Marine slowly looked Grimaldi up and down. "I'm told that you have Harrier time." He made the statement sound like a question.

"I do. And I also have time in Tomcats, F-16s, F-15s and damned near anything else you'd care to mention."

"You'd better have," the Marine said. "Screwing up in a Harrier can get you dead real fast. It's a good plane, but it's not your usual ride."

"I'll keep that in mind."

Grimaldi let his eyes wander over the gray camouflaged fighter. The Marine AV-8B Harrier II wasn't the same jump jet as the ones the British navy had taken to war over the Falkland Islands—it was better. To increase its ordnance and fuel load, the 8B had a fifty percent larger, supercritical, carbon-fiber wing. It also had larger fuel tanks built into the wing, more hard points to carry weapons and even more fuel tanks if needed.

The avionics and fire-control systems were state-of-the-art. An internal navigation system ran both the Heads Up Display—HUD—and a low-level, terrain-following moving map. A laser range finder had been added to ensure even better on-target delivery of the ordnance load.

While this particular Harrier II was a TAV-8B trainer version with twin cockpits, it still had its full armament and ordnance hookups. For this mission, however, most of those underwing hard points would be carrying recon pods instead of bombs and missiles. If trouble came, the two Aden 30 mm cannons mounted on the belly would provide the main defense.

"When do I get my first check ride?" Grimaldi asked.

The Marine glanced at his watch, then over at the ground crew. "They'll be at it for another hour, but we can take her up as soon as they're done."

"Great. Where can I get changed and stow my gear?"

"The ready room's on the other side of the hangar. There's a locker room and a shower."

Bolan checked the time. "The station chief's supposed to be checking in at the DEA flight operations office, so I'll talk to him while you're playing with your new toy."

"Take your time," Grimaldi grinned. "I might be a while."

WHEN BOLAN ARRIVED at the DEA flight operations office at the other end of the field, he found Jim Ransom waiting for him. He gave the station chief a quick rundown, then he and Ransom went over a series of recent satellite photos faxed from Stony Man.

As had been expected, the recon satellite photos were almost useless. Even when the cloud cover allowed a clear shot of the ground below, most of the photos showed only towering jungle. It was true that there were many breaks and clearings in the jungle, but there was nothing that looked like a runway long enough to accommodate a jet fighter.

But as the Executioner had learned from the Harrier briefing, jet fighters didn't necessarily need runways. "Is it possible that they have a jump jet, too?" he asked.

"They could have a space shuttle down there as far as we know." The station chief shrugged. "We just don't know. We haven't gotten diddly out of there for a long time. Every time we send a man up, he makes one or two reports and then vanishes."

Bolan knew how tight security was in the Golden Triangle and knew that there was little the station chief could do about it. "We'll just have to try to find the aircraft ourselves."

"If there's nothing else, Belasko," Ransom said, holding out his hand, "I've got to get back to Bangkok. My people here can get me any time of the day or night."

Bolan shook his hand "I'll keep you informed of anything we find."

Ransom hadn't told Bolan about Brad Winston and his plan to interdict the heroin shipments on the ground because he hadn't seen a connection between that operation and what the special agents were doing. His office conducted many operations that the special agents didn't need to know about.

ONCE MORE Kuhn Sa proved that very little went on in Thailand without his knowing about it. He had been informed of Brad Winston's plan from the very beginning.

Thai special-forces Major Phem was above reproach, as were the majority of his handpicked company of soldiers who were to participate in the operation. The company clerk in his office, however, was not. This corporal had a young wife who enjoyed the finer things in life, things that weren't available to the average corporal in the Thai army, even a corporal in the relatively well-paid special forces.

The money the clerk made passing information to Kuhn Sa's informers allowed him to buy these things for his young and very pretty wife. In return, she didn't leave him for a richer man. Before long he would have enough extra money to buy his wife the latest Japanese electronic toy she wanted. In return, she would submit to him as a wife should, and he wouldn't have to beg for her favors.

As far as the clerk was concerned, it was a low-risk deal and the benefits were well worth what few risks there were.

Passing on word of his major's pending operation took less than five seconds on his way to lunch at the soup shop on the corner. He didn't even get a good look at the face of the shoe-shine boy who took the note from his clenched hand as he walked past.

A steaming bowl of beef-noodle soup and a cold beer later, he had almost forgotten about his betrayal.

3

When Kuhn Sa first learned of Brad Winston's plan to interdict one of his aerial heroin deliveries, the drug lord had a tough decision to make. So far, the only enemies who knew about the Russian Yak VSTOL fighter he'd acquired were dead. And the longer he kept it a secret, the more effective it would be. He wasn't naive enough to think that a single jet fighter, not even one as innovative as the Yak, could long survive an all-out search-and-destroy mission aimed against it. His best defense was to keep it a secret.

Winston's plan was a danger that had to be met, but he had to balance concealing the fighter against the benefits that would be gained by putting the fear of sure sudden death into the minds of his American DEA tormentors. In the end the need to teach a harsh lesson to the Drug Enforcement Administration and its Thai allies won out over keeping the Yak under cover.

He didn't care what the American government did to block heroin shipments from coming into their own country—that was none of his concern. Once he made his deliveries, he didn't bother with what happened to the drug. Waging war on him in his own territory was another matter entirely. The Americans had left him no choice but to remind them whom they were dealing with. He hadn't gotten where he was by being soft on his enemies.

Orders were quickly flashed to Major Lim to have the Russian pilot prepare his fighter for an attack. The impetuous American DEA agent was going to learn that it didn't pay to cross the lord of the Golden Triangle.

WHEN MAJOR LIM BROUGHT Kuhn Sa's attack order, Yuri Galan immediately got to work supervising the preparation of his VSTOL fighter for the ground-attack mission. While he had live-fire, ground-attack experience in Su-22s over the Georgian Republic, he hadn't yet flown the jump jet against ground targets.

This time he had the crew chief arm the Yak with more than air-to-air missiles. Two of his underwing pylons were fitted with Red Chinese copies of the UB-32, 32-round, 57 mm rocket launchers. Though small, the S-5 rockets could be fitted with both armor piercing and antipersonnel warheads. He had fired hundreds of 57 mm shells from his Su-22 and could attest to their effectiveness.

Although the aerial cannons had been designed to attack other fighters, the two GS-301 30 mm weapons in the Yak's belly were also effective ground-attack weapons—particularly when their ammo bays were loaded with straight high-explosive warhead rounds. There would be no need for antipersonnel rounds against human targets.

After the arming was finished, Galan went back to his house for an early dinner. He had a full night's work ahead of him and he liked to go into combat with a full stomach.

BRAD WINSTON STARTED congratulating himself before his interdiction mission was even an hour old. He had planned the raid perfectly, and it was going like clockwork. It was still a half hour before the drug plane was due to land, but as far as he was concerned, the heroin was already in the bag and his transfer back to Washington in the mail.

If his information was correct, and it had been dead right so far, the plane would be carrying at least two five-hundred-pound containers of high-grade China White. This would put him in the record books for the biggest single-agent drug bust in the DEA's history. He didn't bother counting Major Phem and the Thai troops he had brought with him.

When word of his success got back to Washington, he was sure to be the man of the hour. And he was just as sure that his request for an immediate transfer out of this Asian backwater would be approved. How could the man who had interdicted half a ton of China White be refused anything?

He was a little surprised, though, at how easy the mission had gone so far. After a careful infiltration, the Thai special-forces troops had been able to overwhelm the smugglers at the landing zone without having to fire a shot. Their black-and-green-striped camouflage fatigues had rendered them almost invisible as they slipped through the jungle and surrounded the clearing.

Winston watched as three Thai troopers—now in civilian clothing to masquerade as the smugglers—moved out into the clearing. They spread out in a fifty-foot triangle and lighted their flares, giving the plane the safe-to-land signal.

A single flash of a landing light high in the sky showed that the pilot had spotted the signal. It was going down just as Winston had planned.

The DEA agent pulled the .38-caliber Smith & Wesson Police Special revolver from his holster and held it down at his side. It would be a perfect conclusion to the operation if the pilot resisted arrest and had to be shot. He wouldn't shoot to kill him, of course. He knew the value of a live prisoner. The man could be his ticket to bigger and better things.

YURI GALAN CHECKED his arming panel one last time before making his descent to the scheduled landing zone. In the light of the flares below, he could see the fuel truck and the two pickups waiting to transport the heroin. If, of course, he had been carrying heroin on this run. There was nothing in his two drop tanks except fuel for his return trip. The other two underwing pylons were packing weapons.

Transitioning into vertical flight right over the clearing, Galan went into a hover fifty feet above the ground. He dropped the nose of his fighter until the fuel bowser filled the sights of his HUD display and the red diamond pip was centered on the fuel tank. A single press of the control-stick trigger sent a brace of 57 mm rockets streaking for the tanker truck.

Before they struck, the pilot hit his maneuvering thrust-vent controls, and the hovering Yak fighter spun on its axis to line up on the two cargo trucks. More deadly rockets lanced from the Yak's underwing pods just as the fuel truck exploded. Suddenly the light from the torches was lost in the glare of burning jet fuel.

Brad Winston didn't even notice the warm wetness soaking the crotch of his pants and running down his legs. He was too busy trying to get his paralyzed muscles under control long enough to tell his legs to run. As his dreams of glory went up in a ball of fire, the young agent was too stunned to even wonder what had gone wrong with his wonderful, self-serving plan.

In the light of the burning trucks, Galan had no trouble spotting the Thai troops surrounding the clearing. Alternating between his 30 mm belly cannon and the 57 mm rockets, he spun the hovering Yak in a circle, spraying death and destruction into the jungle.

After the first sweep of the clearing, the Russian decided that he wanted some airspeed behind him before he finished the job. He had tempted fate by remaining at a hover as long as he had. Even though there had been no ground fire directed at him so far, he was all too aware of what the American fliers called the "Golden BB." A single rifle bullet in the wrong place could ruin his whole day.

He hit his thrust-vectoring control and slammed the throttle back against the stop. The jet rocketed forward on full power from the thundering R-79V turbine, reaching three hundred miles per hour in a few seconds. Easing back on the stick, the Russian pilot hit his afterburner and sent the Yak screaming for altitude. Once out of small-arms range, he eased off the burner, went into a hard bank and nosed back down onto the clearing in a shallow dive.

This time he chose his targets carefully. With the rocket pods selected for single shot fire, he sent the 57 mm HE projectiles screaming into the wood line around the clearing. The flash of each detonation illuminated more figures in the clearing.

On the ground there was no place to hide. Some of the Thais tried to take the jet out with M-16 fire, but it was to no effect. Most simply ran for their lives.

Brad Winston had finally recovered enough of his faculties to remember how to run himself. But with his pounding heart and the rocket explosions sounding loudly in his ears, he didn't hear the rocket that blew him into bloody fragments. It was traveling at supersonic speed when it took him high in the middle of the back.

The resistance of the agent's spinal column was enough to trigger the warhead's nose fuze, and the round detonated inside his chest cavity.

An observer would have seen the upper half of Winston's body dissolve in a flame-shot, bloody froth. His legs and hips seemed to continue running for an instant before toppling to the ground.

Winston would make the DEA record books as he had so badly wanted, but it wouldn't be on the hero's list. His name would forever be enshrined in the over-ambitious section, with four stars by his name.

KUHN SA WAS PLEASED when he received the radio report of the results of Galan's attack against the DEA. The Americans would think twice before they tried something like that again. It was also good that the losses among the Thai special-forces unit had been so high. Maybe they would also think twice before agreeing to such joint operations in the future.

Now that that problem had been taken care of, the drug lord could turn his thoughts to a report of a new aircraft at Nakhon Phanom. The Americans had sent a jet fighter after him this time, a Harrier, as it was reportedly called. From the information he had received from the agent who had watched it land, it was a jump jet, too, which meant that it was even more dangerous to him than the big surveillance plane had been.

It was obvious that the Americans were planning to bring war to him, and force would be met with force. He was confident that the Russian and his high-tech Yak fighter could deal with this new threat, as well. But Kuhn Sa was still an old jungle warrior, and he knew that it was always best to have two strings for one's bow. There would be no Harrier menacing his operation if it was taken out at its home base before it had a chance to fly against him. As the Yankees said, the best defense was a strong offense.

The air base at Nakhon Phanom was well guarded, but his agents were also well placed. The only problem would be the American security force that was reportedly guarding the hangar where the plane was being stored. His spies told him that there were twenty Marines on duty, with small arms and three or four light machine guns.

That was a sizable force to defend only one hangar, but Kuhn Sa could send three times as many men against them if he had to. The problem was that it would expose too much of his network to Thai police retaliation. It might be better to send in only a small, heavily armed team at night.

Although he planned to destroy the Harrier on the ground, he was going to tell the Russian pilot of this new threat as soon as he landed. As the second string, Galan would have to be prepared to do battle with the Harrier if the ground attack failed.

4

Bolan wasn't pleased when Jim Ransom returned to Nakhon Phanom and told him about the Winston fiasco. It was unfortunate that the young DEA agent had gotten himself killed, but in his line of work, blind ambition often carried a price tag. In Winston's case, he paid top price. What concerned the Executioner was the fact that the station chief hadn't told him that the operation had been planned. Had the warrior known about it, he would have immediately vetoed it. The last thing he needed was for the drug lords to know that he was after their renegade fighter.

"What's done is done," he told Ransom. "But if any more of your men are planning operations like that, you will stop them immediately. Until my operation is successfully completed, there will be no more cowboy stunts. Understand?"

"Yes, sir."

Ransom's contact with the States had left no doubt in his mind about the status of the two special agents. He had been told to place himself and his office under Belasko's orders until their mission was concluded. Even then, he knew he'd be lucky to be allowed to remain with the agency long enough to collect his pension.

"It wasn't a complete blowout, though," Grimaldi said as he read over the reports from the survivors of the Winston debacle. "At least now we know what kind of fighter they're flying,"

Major Phem and the handful of Thai special-forces troopers who had managed to survive the attack had all described the same jet fighter—a long fuselage with short, swept-back wings and twin tails. Even in the hellstorm that had been unleashed on the jungle clearing, their attacker's image had been etched into their memories.

"So you think it's that Russian jump-jet fighter." Bolan frowned. "What did you call it, a Freehand?"

"The Yak-141B, NATO-code-named Freehand," Grimaldi reminded him. "There are only two jump-jet designs in operation right now, and the only one that has twin tails is the Freehand. The thing I can't figure is where in the hell they got it. That craft's supposed to still be in flight testing."

"The drug lords of the Golden Triangle have enough money to buy anything they want and the Russians are in a selling mood right now."

"My question, sir," Ransom said cautiously, "is how the hell did they get it down here from Moscow?"

Grimaldi shrugged. "That's no sweat. All they needed to do was arrange for a couple of refuelings along the way. It's a long flight, but the pilot can use the relief tube. Call it five thousand miles. With drop tanks, that's only two refueling stops."

Bolan brought the conversation back to the topic foremost in his mind. "Are you going to have any trouble dealing with this guy if it comes to a dog-fight?"

"I think I can handle him," Grimaldi said confidently. "The Yak-141B is fast, sure, but, it's not supposed to be as maneuverable as the Harrier II. It would be more than a match for most conventional fighters, but I don't think it will do quite as well against another jump jet. Particularly ours."

"You'd better be right about that."

The pilot grinned. "Since I'm going to be in the front seat, you can bet your sweet ass I'm right, 'cause I'll be betting mine."

"This does add a twist to the mission, though."

"Not really. We knew we were looking for some kind of fighter. Now that we know exactly what it is, it makes dealing with it a little easier."

"But," Bolan said, "since it's a jump jet, it can land almost anywhere."

"Almost anyplace a medium-size helicopter can land, right."

Bolan shook his head. "There are a lot of clearings that size in that jungle."

"We'll find it. I've got faith in that Harrier recon package. If it's down there, we'll be able to pick it up on at least one of the sensors."

"Just as long as we find it before it finds us."

Grimaldi laid his arm over his friend's shoulder. "Piece of cake. Ol' Smiling Jack isn't going to let any Russian get the drop on him. I don't care what he's flying."

"Regardless," Bolan replied, "I want us to move into the hangar with those Marines until we're ready to go. Somebody's got a line into the Bangkok DEA office, and they might know about us, as well. I don't want anything happening to that plane."

WHEN YURI GALAN WAS TOLD about the Harrier, he realized that the Americans had brought in the fighter specifically to hunt him down. It made sense. The best weapon to use to fight a jump jet was another one.

Unfortunately for the Americans, even a Harrier II TAV-8B, which he believed this one to be, wasn't a match for the Yak-141B. For a second-generation VSTOL fighter, the Harrier II was a capable aircraft. His Yak-141B Freehand, however, was a third-generation jump jet, and in fighter design, a single generation was a great leap forward.

The original Yak-141 prototypes would have been able to take on a Harrier II in a dogfight and best it most of the time. The B model should be able to do it ninety-nine percent of the time thanks to its greatly improved maneuverability. The small canard wings fitted to the sides of the B model's air intakes were the secret to that.

Using vectored thrust as an aid in aerial maneuvering—vectoring in flight, as it was called—had been termed "viffing" by the British. The Harrier "viffed" by swiveling its four thrust nozzles in conjunction with its conventional control surfaces. This was what had given the British jump jet its high kill ratio over the Falkland Islands.

Since the Yak-141 used lift engines in the front of the fuselage for vertical thrust and had only a single swiveling thrust nozzle in the tail, it couldn't viff in flight like a Harrier. To make up for that dogfight deficiency, the Yakovlev designers borrowed an American design feature and added small canard control surfaces on the sides of the air intakes forward of the wings. When these were turned in conjunction with the rear nozzle, the canards allowed the fighter to "turn on a dime and spit out nine cents change." There hadn't been such a maneuverable fighter since the days of the Red Baron and his Fokker triplane.

This would be Galan's first opportunity to match his piloting skills against another fighter pilot. Shooting down helicopters and spy planes didn't count. Fighter pilots lived to pit their skills against a worthy adversary in aerial combat, and he was looking forward to the test.

He regretted being in the jungle, however, instead of at a Russian air force base where he would have had access to detailed information about his potential adversary. Knowing more about your opponent's fighter than he knew about yours gave a pilot a critical edge that could mean the difference between life and death.

He mentioned this need for information to Major Lim, and the next day a helicopter delivered a package to him, along with a resupply of missiles and ammunition for the Yak. Inside the package was a stack of magazines and books relating to the Harrier and its use in combat during the Falkland Islands and Gulf wars. Most of the books and magazines were in English, but the general had thoughtfully provided him with a Russian-English dictionary.

The most impressive thing about the Harrier's performance in the Falklands conflict was its kill ratio against the Argentinean air force. The South Americans had been flying some pretty good fighters, Mirage IIIs and A-4 Skyhawks, but the Harriers had been able to down more than thirty of them with no losses to themselves.

Even considering that the British were probably far better pilots than the Argentineans, it was an impressive record and spoke volumes about the agile jump jet. And the version of the fighter the Americans were reported to be flying was even better. Since it was a TAV-8B, it would be an even more worthy opponent.

After a day of translation and study, Galan felt that he knew as much as he needed to know about his future opponent's fighter. The other thing he needed to know, he would have to wait to find out. The only to determine the other pilot's courage and skill was to meet him in aerial combat.

DUSK WAS FALLING when Bolan and Grimaldi took Marine Gunnery Sergeant Minery with them on an inspection of the hangar's perimeter defenses. The veteran sergeant wasn't happy about having to explain the deployment of his troops to civilians, even DEA civilians. But Captain Jenson had told him to play along with these guys, and so he would.

It didn't take the Marine long, however, to realize that these two DEA agents had military experience in their past, particularly the big dark-haired guy. Belasko had the eye of a combat company commander and he sure as hell knew his weapons.

"Do you have any warning or listening devices covering that open area, Sergeant?" Bolan looked out at the two hundred yards of tall grass between the north side of the hangar and the perimeter fence.

"We don't have any with us, sir," the sergeant answered. "All I was told was that we'd be securing a hangar within a secured air base. Our authorized load for this kind of mission doesn't have any ground sensors in it."

Bolan had been around the military long enough to know better than to blame the sergeant for doing only what was authorized. The fault was with whoever had drawn up the authorized-load list.

"What coordination have you made with the Thai air police?" Grimaldi asked.

"Not much," he admitted. "I have a land line to the desk sergeant in their ready room and their vehicle patrol schedule. They also have a platoon-size ready reaction force standing by during the hours of darkness."

The Executioner pointed toward the perimeter. "I'd like you to put out a couple of two-man listening posts with radios at least a hundred yards away from the hangar. Let the Thais know that you're putting them out there, but don't let them talk you out of it."

Now the sergeant was confused. This was supposed to be a simple job of keeping unauthorized people out of the hangar, not a combat assignment. "Do you have some information about a threat that I don't have, sir?"

"No, but considering what happened to the last DEA plane that operated out of this base, I don't want to take any chances."

"Yes, sir."

"Also," Bolan added, "I want Grimaldi and myself issued M-16s when we get back to the hangar."

"We don't have any extra weapons with us, sir."

"We'll just borrow them from the mechanics, okay? They'll be working on the Harrier tonight and won't need them."

The sergeant shrugged. "Yes, sir."

THE LEADER OF KUHN SA'S eight-man strike team kept his head down and his eyes closed as the Thai air-police vehicle passed on the other side of the perimeter fence. The APs went by quickly and probably didn't even look at the fence as they drove past. This was the second time he had hidden and watched to see how they conducted their patrols.

As soon as the vehicle was gone, he took the padded wire cutters from his belt. Crawling the last three meters to the chain-link fence, he quickly cut a flap big enough to admit a man's body. Holding the wire open, he motioned for the men behind him to slip through.

One by one, the raiders silently slipped through the fence and dashed across the inner perimeter road to hide in the tall grass on the other side. When they were all through, the leader pulled the chain-link wire back down and tied it in place with a twist of rice straw. That would hold the flap down, but would break away easily if they had to get back through in a hurry.

Two hundred meters in front of them, the hangar was brightly lit with security lights all the way around it. But the cone of light extended only fifteen meters or so from the hangar walls. Beyond that, the field was in darkness. With their hands and faces covered with charcoal, and wearing black peasant clothes and head rags, the raiders were nearly invisible in the moonless night.

Their leader stopped and smelled the air. Over the jet-engine kerosene fumes and motor-vehicle exhaust of the air base, he smelled something completely out of place. When he recognized the odor, he smiled to himself. There were American sentries out there and one of them was wearing a strong, spicy after-shave lotion. Only Westerners would wear perfume while standing guard.

He lowered himself to the ground, then raised his head until his eyes were level with the knee-high grass. Though it was a moonless night, the sky was lighter than the surrounding terrain, so he would be able to see all shapes and movement against the sky.

It took but a moment to spot the sentries. The distinctive silhouettes of two men wearing American combat helmets showed against the sky. He watched long enough to see that there were only those two.

Making the cry of a female cricket, he called two of his men to his side. After pointing out the Americans' position, he motioned for them to take out the sentries. He loosened his long machete in its sheath and continued to watch the Yankees while his men moved in on them. If something went wrong, he would try to take them out without starting a firefight.

There was the faintest rustle in the grass. The two helmets disappeared. The leader waited to hear the signal before moving forward again.

When he crawled past the bodies of the two Americans, he smiled. If those were the best the Americans could find to guard their airplane, it was as good as destroyed.

5

The cones of brightness thrown by the security lights on the hangar's roof cast deep shadows in the open areas beyond their reach. When Bolan stepped out of the building, he squinted into their glare and shifted his grip on the M-16/M-203 over-and-under rifle and grenade launcher he had borrowed from a Marine mechanic. Along with the assault rifle, he had the field belt with the two magazine pouches buckled around his waist and the three bandoliers of 40 mm grenades slung over his shoulder.

The fact that the renegade jump jet had attacked the DEA ambush didn't necessarily mean that the Harrier was endangered. It wasn't a good sign, however. Obviously the drug lords were one step ahead of them this time and had been since the beginning. Since that was the case, a prudent man would be expecting trouble, and if Bolan was anything, he was prudent.

After warning the two Marines in the machine-gun bunker on the northwest corner of the hangar that he was heading out, Bolan moved forward into the darkness. He stayed close enough to the hangar so as not to run into the two-man team the sergeant had put on patrol.

As soon as the Executioner was out of the light, he stopped and went to ground to give his eyes a chance to adjust to the darkness. Once he could see clearly, he scanned the open area in front of him. When it was clear, he moved laterally in front of the hangar stopping every now and then to listen to the night sounds.

Suddenly he stopped and crouched in the darkness. The crickets had stopped chirping. Something out there had disturbed their song, and that something was an intruder. He was bringing the radio up to his mouth to warn Sergeant Minery when the night was shattered by the brilliant back blast of an RPG-7 antitank rocket launcher.

Bolan instinctively swung the muzzle of his M-16 toward the launcher as he went flat on his face on the tarmac. The 85 mm rocket streaked past him and hit the side of the hangar.

The armor-piercing warhead cut through the thin sheet-metal wall as if it were paper. The sheet metal did deflect the rocket's path downward, however, so that it hit the floor and detonated. The antitank warhead blasted chunks of concrete from the floor and sent them flying with the force. One of the Marine mechanics took a hit in the leg and went down.

Blinking his eyes to banish the back-blast flare of the RPG launcher from his vision, Bolan saw the shadowy shapes of two men kneeling in the grass a hundred yards distant. One of them raised the launcher to his shoulder to fire again.

A flick of the Executioner's thumb sent the M-16's selector switch to full-auto as his finger tightened on the trigger. A long burst of 5.56 mm slugs brought a scream from one of the men, the loader. The man with the launcher swung the weapon toward Bolan, who could see the rocket warhead loaded into its muzzle and ready to fire.

The RPG-7 had been designed as an tank buster, but the warrior knew firsthand that it was also an effective antipersonnel weapon. He triggered the 40 mm grenade launcher under the barrel of his rifle and rolled out of the gunner's line of fire.

The grenade landed in front of the RPG gunner and exploded into dozens of tiny, razor sharp fragments. The shrapnel scythed through the air, slicing deep into him.

Right on the heels of the grenade's detonation, the Marine guards in the machine-gun bunker opened fire. A long burst of 7.62 mm rounds from their M-60 finished the job Bolan had started.

The dying Thai's trigger finger spasmed and the RPG fired. Fortunately the gunner had been going down as the rocket's prop charge ignited, and the launcher was pulled off target. The rocket streaked for the sky, missing the roof of the hangar by several feet.

Bolan heard shouts behind him as the Marine sergeant raced out of the hangar with ten of his troops at his heels. A burst of AK fire from the darkness cut down one of the Marines in midstride. The others went to ground and immediately returned fire.

"Minery," Bolan called over the radio, "this is Belasko. I'm on your right flank, fifty yards out. I got the

RPG gunner and his loader, but I don't know how many of them are still out there. Over."

"Roger. I'm bringing the other squad up to reinforce us."

"Cancel that," Bolan ordered. "Leave them where they are in case this is a feint."

"Right, sir."

As Bolan watched, the Marines broke up into two fire teams and moved out to his right. Now that the element of surprise had been lost, the attackers opened up on the Marines. The clatter of their AKs was answered by the faster-firing M-16s and the distinctive thump of the M-203 grenade launchers.

Bolan slammed another 40 mm grenade into the breech of his launcher. Rolling over onto his belly, he lined the sights up on the muzzle-flashes of two AKs and triggered his weapon. The detonation was followed by a scream of pain as more of the deadly shrapnel struck home.

Now that the Marines were working out, Bolan held his fire so as not to hit one of them in the dark. When a parachute flare rocketed up into the sky and burst over the grassy area, he saw that the battle was almost over. The Marines were advancing, their M-16s blazing fire.

THE LEADER of the raiding party had managed to crawl unseen to within fifteen meters of the hangar. Through the blasted hole in the wall, he could see the jet fighter he had come to destroy, and it looked to be undamaged.

Though he had never met Kuhn Sa, he'd worked for the drug lord for many years. He had been recruited while in jail awaiting trial on a smuggling charge. The day after pledging his life and loyalty to Kuhn Sa, the charges against him had been dropped and he walked out of prison a free man. But none of Kuhn Sa's army of agents and spies were really free. All of them lived or died at the drug lord's whim.

He knew what would be in store for him if he failed to complete his mission. What was even more important was that he knew what would be in store for his wife and five children. Were he to live to report his failure, his family would share his punishment. If he died, however, they would be well taken care of. Kuhn Sa excused failures if you died while you were trying to succeed.

Mouthing a silent prayer for Buddha to grant him a better life the next time around, he jumped to his feet and charged for the hole in the wall of the hangar. Firing his AK on full auto with one hand as he ran, he used the other to grasp the friction detonator for the satchel charge.

Bolan saw the suicide run and recognized the satchel charge clutched to the man's chest. Dropping to one knee, he flicked the M-16's selector to semiauto as he tried to line up the sights for a difficult head shot. A body shot could detonate the satchel charge.

When his first shot missed, he switched back to full-auto and, sighting low, swept the man's legs out from under him with a long, magazine-emptying burst.

Even though his arms were still pumping, his shattered legs wouldn't support him and the running man went down. Turning his face toward Bolan, he reached down to his chest. An instant later, a flash of light and a cloud of flame-shot smoke marked the place where the man had chosen death over paying the price of failure.

The Thai had been only twenty feet away when the satchel charge detonated, and Bolan was blown onto his back from the force of the explosion.

The Executioner was getting to his feet when three Thai air-police vehicles screamed up to the front of the hangar and slammed to a halt. A dozen APs in flak vests and steel pots jumped out with their M-16s at the ready, but it was all over.

Now that the threat was ended for the moment, Bolan let the Marine captain and the gunnery sergeant deal with the Thai air police.

He walked back into the hangar to check on the Harrier.

"WELL," GRIMALDI SAID as he surveyed the holes in the hanger walls after the air police left. "I think we can safely assume that they know we're coming for them."

"I think that's pretty much a foregone conclusion," Bolan agreed. "Hal wanted this operation to be kept low-profile, but it looks like the opposition knows what we're doing here."

The Marine captain hurried up to them with a report. "The Thai base security officer has pulled in more troops," he said. "They'll be covering us for the rest of the night and will beef up security tomorrow."

"How many men did you lose?" Bolan asked. He had seen at least two go down.

The Marine officer's face was grim. "I have three men dead and half a dozen wounded." He paused as if searching for words. "I sure as hell hope this operation of yours is worth it, mister."

They were more numbers to add to the butcher's bill, a bill that Bolan intended to see paid one way or the other. "It is, Captain," he answered simply.

"Was the Harrier damaged?" Grimaldi changed the subject.

The Marine shook his head. "Other than a couple of paint chips. My men haven't found any damage yet. But I'm having them run a full diagnostic check on all the systems just to make sure."

"How long will that take?" Bolan asked.

"Three or four hours."

"Let me know as soon as they're done," Grimaldi said. "We need to fly that mission tomorrow while we still can."

"Yes, sir."

Waiting until the Marine was out of earshot, Bolan spoke softly. "I want to let Hal know what went down here and then we'd both better try to get some sleep. They won't be coming back tonight."

"How about tomorrow night?"

"We'll worry about that tomorrow night. But I don't think anyone will be getting through the fence again.

The Thais lost face here tonight, and they'll be out in force to make sure it doesn't happen again.''

''Maybe they'll try to take us out with a suicide car bomb next time.''

''There's always that.''

IN THE MORNING, Bolan and Grimaldi changed into their flight gear and walked into the damaged hangar. Captain Jenson was waiting for them near the Harrier.

''She's ready,'' the Marine said proudly. ''I've had the whole nine yards checked and rechecked. The diagnostics for the internal nav gear, the terrain-following radar, the fire-control system, laser range finder and the sensor packages are all reading out a hundred percent.''

''Let's take a look,'' Grimaldi said.

Despite what Jenson said about everything being checked and double-checked, he made a walk-around inspection. Any pilot who failed to do that deserved what was going to happen to him sooner or later.

Two AIM-9L Sidewinder missiles were hanging on the outer pylons of both wings and the other three hard points were taken up with the sensors. Side Looking Radar—SLR—MAD and infrared cameras had all been mounted. With all those sensor packages, if it was possible to see it from the air, Grimaldi would spot it.

''She looks good to me,'' he told Bolan as he put on his flight helmet. ''Let's get this show on the road.''

While Grimaldi carefully ran through his start-up checklist in the front cockpit, Bolan strapped himself into the rear cockpit and plugged the intercom cord from his helmet into the radio jack.

"Commo check." Grimaldi's voice came over Bolan's earphones. "How do you hear me?"

"I've got you loud and clear, Jack."

"I'm lighting the burner now."

The Rolls-Royce Pegasus 11 turbine ignited with a whoosh and the smell of burning kerosene. The watching Marine mechanics protected their ears from the roar of the turbine reverberating inside the closed hangar.

As soon as all the instrument readouts were in the green, Grimaldi motioned with his hands and the Marines slid the huge hangar doors open. Coming off the brakes, he taxied out onto the sun-baked tarmac. Before he had gone more than a plane length, he had the canopy slid shut and the cockpit air conditioner on full blast.

Although the Harrier could take off vertically with the load she was carrying, Grimaldi taxied the jet onto the runway for a short-length, rolling takeoff. It saved wear and tear on both the turbine and the tarmac.

Stopping at the end of the runway, he dropped his flaps to full position and stood on the brakes while he ran the engine up to full rpm. With one last glance at his instrument panel, he came off the brakes, slammed the throttle forward and the jet quickly accelerated down the tarmac. By the time the Harrier had gone five plane lengths, it was moving at almost two hundred miles per hour.

"Hang on back there," Grimaldi called out over the intercom. "We're jumping now."

When he hit the controls to swivel the thrust nozzles down, the Harrier zoomed into the air as if a helicopter rotor were attached to the top of the fuselage. It was quite a sensation to be in slow flight and still climbing at a forty-five-degree angle.

Once the jump jet was five hundred feet in the air, Grimaldi swiveled the thrust nozzles all the way to the rear and the Harrier quickly picked up speed. A few seconds later, he banked up on one wing and aimed the fighter's nose for the northeast and the Golden Triangle.

"Look out, Freehand," he called out over the intercom, "we're coming at ya."

"Not yet," Bolan said. "We're supposed to be looking for the wreckage of that surveillance plane first. We'll go after the Yak later."

"Just as long as I get a chance at it."

6

The Harrier's takeoff from Nakhon Phanom didn't pass unnoticed. As Kuhn Sa had proved the night before, the Thai air force base wasn't beyond the reach of his hands and eyes. The same spies who had reported the comings and goings of the ill-fated DEA E-3 surveillance plane, had also kept their controllers informed of the Harrier's arrival and its activities.

The warning that the Harrier was taking off from the Thai air base with full underwing loads reached Yuri Galan's makeshift airfield within minutes. Kuhn Sa's Intelligence network included a state-of-the-art communications and retransmission system that was the nerve center of his operation. Every one of his agent controllers in the towns and cities had access to a radio that could reach the drug lord's remote mountain sanctuary.

"Galan!" Major Lim shouted as he ran toward the Russian pilot's house. "Get in the air. We have received word that the Yankees are coming. They took off from Nakhon Phanom fifteen minutes ago."

"I hear you," Galan shouted back. "I'm on the way."

The Russian smiled as he ran for his fighter. He had been looking forward to this aerial confrontation with the Americans. Since first being alerted to fly against the Harrier, Galan had been living in his flight suit. All he had to do was zip it up, slip into his gloves and grab his helmet as he ran for the Yak's concealed parking spot under the trees.

The Chinese ground crew was stripping the camouflage netting off the jet, and the crew chief was already in the cockpit firing up the turbines. When he saw the pilot running toward him, he evacuated the cockpit and waited to help Galan buckle himself in.

The pilot climbed into the cockpit seat, his eyes scanning the instrument readings while his practiced hands buckled his parachute harness and plugged in his flight suit's anti-g force and radio connections. After doing a double check, the crew chief gave him a thumbs-up before dropping to the ground. With a last look at the turbine instruments, Galan closed and locked the canopy.

Not wanting to waste precious time while the ground crew pushed the Yak out from under the trees, Galan impatiently motioned for them to get out of the way. When he saw that they were all in the clear, he eased off the brakes and advanced the throttle, letting the jet thrust push the fighter out into the cleared landing zone.

As soon as the crew chief signaled that he was clear of all obstacles, Galan locked the brakes. Opening the jet's intake door on the top of the fuselage, he swiveled the rear nozzle down and advanced the jet's throttle to a hundred percent thrust. With an ear-splitting roar, the fighter lifted off the ground.

The landing zone had been watered down to try to hold the dust against the jet's blast, but swirls of small debris billowed below the Yak. Fortunately the jet quickly broke free of the ground effect and was clear of the flying junk.

As soon as Galan broke into clean air above the treetops, he retracted his landing gear and swung his rear-jet nozzle to the forward thrust position. When the Yak started accelerating, he closed off the lift intake and cut the fuel to the lift-jet turbines.

Now that the airframe was clean, Galan let out all the stops. Going into afterburner, the Yak broke Mach unity under the thirty-four thousand pounds of screaming thrust. Galan pointed the nose almost straight up, climbing for altitude and heading for his rendezvous with a fighter pilot's destiny.

In aerial combat, speed and altitude were the most important factors in the opening engagement. If you had those two things working for you, you had a good chance of winning. Since the Russian fully intended to come out the victor in his first man-to-man aerial encounter, he was taking no chances. Leveling out at twenty thousand feet, he banked away to the south.

Ten minutes later he was in position to intercept the American intruder when it reached the Golden Triangle. Leaving his radar turned off so as not to warn him, Galan scanned the sky. Even from six thousand meters, he had no trouble spotting the Harrier. The American fighter's two-tone gray-camouflage paint scheme stood out against the deep greens of the jungle as if it had lights shining on it.

While he had "look down-shoot down" capability in his fire-control system, the Russian didn't want to end the fight with his first shot. For this to be a real fighter-pilot-to-fighter-pilot dogfight, he had to let the American know that he was coming so he'd have a chance to defend himself. Anything less would not do.

Reaching out with a gloved hand, he flicked on his gun-laying radar as he nosed over into a dive.

"WE'RE ENTERING the search area in zero five," Grimaldi called back to Bolan in the rear cockpit.

"Roger," Bolan answered. "I'll get the sensors up and running."

The warrior reached out and switched on the SLR, the MAD detector and the IR imager. He also engaged the terrain-following and mapping radar along with the camera pod. No matter what they found on this recon mission, with the in-flight recorders backing up all the sensor equipment, at least they would have a record of it.

"Everything's in the green and we're recording."

"Roger."

Suddenly a shriek sounded in Grimaldi's earphones. The tail-mounted threat detector had picked up the Russian's aerial targeting radar.

"He's on us!" the pilot shouted as he slammed the throttle up against the stop and pulled back on the control stick.

Nose up, the Harrier clawed for altitude. Like the Russian, Grimaldi knew that altitude and airspeed were the keys to victory, and he had let himself get caught flying low and slow. With the enemy fighter on his tail, he had to get some height or they would die before he even had a chance to fight.

As Grimaldi climbed, Bolan turned in his seat and scanned the sky above them for the bogie. He caught a flash high in the sky behind them and to their rear. "Break! He's on your six!"

ON HIS WAY DOWN, Galan decided not to fire on his initial pass. He was so confident of his ability to take out the Harrier that he wanted to give the American pilot a chance to show what he could do in a dogfight. He kept his finger on the control-stick trigger, though, as he dived on the Harrier. Galan was still supersonic when he flashed past the enemy jet and pulled up in front of it in a steep climb.

"He missed us," Bolan said.

"He didn't fire," Grimaldi replied. "But I'm not going to give the bastard a break."

The instant the pipper diamond in Grimaldi's HUD target display blinked red, he triggered the AIM-9L Sidewinder from the port wing.

The missile dropped off the port-side pylon and instantly ignited. Trailing a plume of dirty white smoke, it streaked for the Yak.

The jet's threat system picked up Grimaldi's launch. With the missile-launch warning screaming in his earphones, Galan waited to make his move. At the last possible moment, he hit the vectoring-nozzle control and slammed the stick hard over to the right side. With the nozzle of the thirty-five-thousand-pound thrust R-79V turbojet pointed up, the forward canards turned down and the ailerons in full lock for a right-hand roll, the Freehand was no longer where it had been in the sky.

Galan continued his abrupt, climbing snap roll to the right, and Grimaldi's Sidewinder passed harmlessly through the clear blue sky where the Russian fighter had been only a split second before.

"Oh, shit," Grimaldi muttered softly when he saw his missile miss the Yak by well over a hundred yards. He'd had a lock on, and the Sidewinder had been running true, but none of that mattered against a jump jet that could simply step out of the way. This wasn't going to be the foregone conclusion he'd thought it would be. If he wanted this guy, he was going to have to work for it.

Galan held his Yak in the tight turn until his nose was pointed back in the direction of the American's Harrier. Now it was his turn.

Grimaldi was transfixed as he watched the Yak's maneuver. Whoever was flying that fighter was good, maybe a little too good. The Yak's tactical-maneuvering envelope seemed to be a high-speed program, though, and maybe he could use that against him.

He still had his four vectoring nozzles and the Harrier's famous viffing tactics. Viffing was a relatively low-speed maneuver, but it might work. It wouldn't be the first time that a slower fighter shot down a faster opponent. Even propeller-driven Navy A-1 "Super Spad" attack bombers had shot down MiG jet fighters in Vietnam.

The Russian pilot now selected his belly-mounted 30 mm cannon, rather than try a missile on his first attack. He set the rate-of-fire selector for a quarter-second burst. The instant the pipper in the HUD display turned red, Galan triggered the 30 mm and watched the green tracers streak across the sky toward the enemy jet.

He'd had a good sight picture, and the Yak was in a skidding turn that should have brought the 30 mm cannon shells right across the American's midsection. Suddenly, though, the Harrier jumped out of his line of fire.

Galan smiled as he saw his tracers miss their intended target. So that was the famous Harrier viffing maneuver he'd read so much about. It was a slick move, he had to admit, but he was confident the Yak could beat it. Reaching down to his armament panel, he started to select one of the Atoll air-to-air missiles for his next shot, but thought better of it.

When he bested this American pilot, he didn't want it to be because of the cold, mechanical circuitry of a missile warhead's guidance system. He wanted to kill this man the old-fashioned way—like a real dogfighter—with the guns mounted in his fighter.

Snapping his canards into the full-up position and the thrust nozzle into full down, Galan caused the Yak to pitch up so abruptly that it was flying forward belly first. He grunted against the brutal g force slamming him against the armored seat, but kept the stick sucked all the way back into his stomach until the Yak was upside down.

When completely inverted, Galan was almost hanging in the air, his forward momentum not yet canceled by the screaming thrust of his engine. The Yak wasn't viffing but had turned completely around in a shorter distance than even the Harrier could accomplish. And its nose was aimed directly at its startled opponent.

Grimaldi saw the Yak coming and hit the vectoring controls again to viff out of the line of fire. But he was slow this time.

When the Harrier flashed past in front of his canopy, Galan pressed the cannon trigger again. The high-velocity 30 mm revolver cannon growled for a preset quarter second. But in that brief time, it sent twenty HE- and AP-tipped shells after the wildly skidding Harrier.

The shell that smashed into the turbine-compressor section of the Harrier's Rolls-Royce jet engine shredded the spinning turbine blades, turning them into twisted, whirling, red-hot shrapnel. Each broken stainless-steel blade carried the destructive power of another 30 mm cannon shell as it ripped through the airframe.

In an instant, the guts of the Harrier were shredded. The jet engine's lube-oil reservoir exploded as a red-hot blade sliced through it. The hydraulic fluid flamed next, just in time to ignite the JP-4 jet fuel spraying out of the ruptured fuel line.

Grimaldi didn't even have time to shout a warning as the instrument panel went crazy. Instead, he slammed his back against the armored seat and jerked hard on the ejection-sequence handle.

The rear seat fired first, blowing an unsuspecting Bolan through the top of the closed canopy. A second later, Grimaldi's seat fired, too, and both men were clear of the doomed Harrier. Seconds later, their automatic releases functioned to separate them from their seats and to pop their parachute canopies open above them.

Freed from Grimaldi's hands on the controls, the doomed Harrier flipped over onto its back and started to come apart in the air as it went into an inverted flat spin. An explosion in the engine bay sent burning debris showering to the jungle below to mark the jet's death.

7

The doomed Harrier hadn't been flying straight and level when Jack Grimaldi hit the ejection-seat initiator to punch them out. The ejection charges had sent both men tumbling through the air, and they had trouble getting their seats to separate cleanly and their parachutes to deploy properly.

When Bolan finally got his chute under control, he watched the flaming debris of the Harrier rain on the jungle below him. As with the earlier DEA planes shot down by the renegade Russian fighter, the jungle canopy opened to swallow the wreckage. As soon as it rained, there would be no sign of the fighter having crashed at all.

Even though the two ejection seats had fired only a few seconds apart, the stricken jump jet had been moving fast enough that Bolan was descending a mile or so away from Grimaldi's canopy. He made a mental note of the pilot's location so they could quickly link up when they reached the ground.

All too soon the jungle seemed to reach up toward him at blinding speed, and Bolan saw that he hadn't been paying enough attention to his impending landing. He pulled hard on the parachute risers, trying to maneuver to what looked like a break in the canopy of trees below.

He almost made it.

Instead, the parachute snagged on a branch some thirty feet above the jungle floor. Snapped to an abrupt halt, Bolan hung in the harness for a moment to make sure that the parachute wasn't going to pull loose and drop him to the ground. When he was satisfied that the canopy was firmly caught in the tree, the warrior twisted in his harness to reach above him for the risers. Climbing the nylon cords as if they were ropes, he made his way up to the main branch. Once he had a secure footing, he unbuckled the parachute harness and let it fall.

The parachute canopy hanging in the tree was a dead giveaway to anyone searching for them from the air, but he didn't bother to pull it down. The opposition already knew where they were.

Making his way to the tree's trunk, the Executioner dropped from one limb to the next until he finally reached the jungle floor. Once on the ground, he took a quick inventory of his surroundings. In Grimaldi's back seat, he had been a passenger during the dogfight that ended with his being blown out of the sky. Now that he was back in his element, he could control his own destiny again.

He had to assume that the pilot of the Russian jet had radioed their crash location to his employers. And if any of the drug lord's troops were in the vicinity, they would close in as fast as they could. Kuhn Sa wouldn't want any survivors escaping to tell tales of his private air force in the jungle.

If he and Grimaldi were to survive, they had to get out of the area fast.

Reaching into the side pocket of his flight suit, Bolan pulled out his survival radio. He switched it on and held the microphone to his mouth. "Jack," he called.

There was no answer, only a hissing of static.

"Jack," he tried again, "can you read me?"

Again, there was no reply.

There could only be two reasons why Grimaldi wasn't answering his calls—either the radio wasn't working or he was in no condition to talk. Whichever one it was, Bolan had to get to the pilot ASAP.

Right before landing in the tree, he had seen the pilot's parachute canopy descending a mile or so to the west. Leaving the survival radio switched over to receive, he put it in the breast pocket of his flight suit and headed in that direction.

THIRTY MINUTES LATER, Bolan had covered only a little more than a half mile in the dense vegetation when he heard the old familiar sound of helicopter rotors in the distance, approaching fast and low.

Taking the time to find a good hiding place, he drew his .44 Magnum Desert Eagle from his shoulder holster and flicked off the safety. As he waited, he heard the chopper go into a hover a few hundred yards to the west. After a few minutes, it flew off to continue the search.

He again tried to call Grimaldi on the radio. But as before, there was no answer.

He was moving out of his hiding place when he heard a triumphant shout a couple hundred yards ahead of him. The first shout was followed by bellowed orders in an Oriental language.

Bolan didn't have to comprehend the language to know what the words meant. They had found Grimaldi before the pilot had found a place to hole up. To his relief, though, no gunfire had sounded. The pilot was being taken prisoner instead of being shot on sight.

A few minutes later, he heard the chopper come back and again go into a hover over the location. After hovering in place long enough to winch up the prisoner and the search team, the rotors changed pitch and the chopper flew away.

The warrior didn't take that to mean that he was safe, however. There was no doubt in his mind that the opposition knew that two men had punched out of the Harrier. The pilot of the Yak would have reported seeing two parachutes in the sky. Whoever had just flown Grimaldi out was sure to have left search teams behind to look for the man who had been wearing that second parachute. Dead or alive, they would want him, too. Plus, his battle-trained instincts told him that he wasn't alone in the jungle.

Nonetheless, he had to check out the situation.

It didn't take him long to find where Grimaldi had been snatched. The sign of a struggle with several men was clear in the crushed vegetation. But there was no blood on the ground, so he might not have been injured. That was about the only good news in this whole thing.

Grimaldi's gear, including the canopy of his chute, had been taken with him. The drug lords wanted no trace of him left behind. They intended that he join the other missing men who had fallen victim to the renegade Russian fighter. The difference was that Grimaldi had a friend who wasn't about to allow him to disappear. The chopper had departed to the northeast, so the Executioner would head in that direction.

He knew the futility of trying to find Grimaldi without a guide. Were he in Bangkok or Rangoon, he could activate his old contacts and probably come up with someone who knew Kuhn Sa's current camps. But the cities were a long distance away, and trying to make his way back to them would be almost as dangerous as following after the chopper.

The deciding factor was that Grimaldi was being held prisoner and had to be rescued ASAP. He could no more leave him behind, even for a couple of days, than he could quit breathing. Regardless of the outcome, he would remain in the jungle until he learned his friend's fate.

First, though, he had to arm and equip himself. That meant that he had to stick around long enough to make contact with one of the search teams looking for him. It would be tricky, but it was necessary. He was completely at home in the jungle, but it was a home that was always more comfortable if you were outfitted properly.

BOLAN'S COMBAT INSTINCTS had been right once again. Search teams had been left behind to look for him, and they weren't amateurs. He barely had time to duck back into cover when he spotted two men coming down the trail.

Both men had their AKs at port arms and were carefully checking the trail for signs as they passed. Bolan sank lower behind his cover, thanking his luck that he hadn't crossed the trail. These men weren't carrying rucksacks, but they had assault rifles and ammunition. If he could take them out, he could equip himself well enough to start the journey to find Grimaldi.

He had the Desert Eagle in his shoulder holster, but firing the big pistol would be a dead giveaway that he was still in the search area. The heavy semiauto had a distinctive boom unlike anything likely to be found in this part of the world. A single shot from the pistol would bring everyone within a mile radius running.

There was, however, the cold steel solution. His Tanto knife was strapped to his boot top. To use it successfully, though, he had to get the two men separated. Trying to take out two armed men with one knife was a little more than he wanted to venture.

The two men unwittingly gave him his opening. One of the soldiers slung his AK over his shoulder and turned off into the brush to take care of personal business, while the other man continued down the trail.

Bolan quickly, but silently, worked his way around behind the first soldier. The man was so intent on emptying his bladder that he didn't hear the warrior approach. Bolan closed the last few feet with a leap, his hand going for the man's mouth as the knife went in low. The razor-sharp chisel point drove through the hardman's flesh and into his right kidney.

The soldier stiffened, but Bolan clamped his hand over his mouth to keep him from crying out. When the man went limp, the Executioner quietly lowered him to the ground and dragged the body farther back under cover.

The warrior snatched up the fallen AK-47 and grabbed a spare magazine from the man's chest pack to stuff into the side pocket of his flight suit. He slowly pulled back on the charging handle of the assault rifle to make sure a round was in the chamber. When he saw the copper gleam of a ChiCom 7.62 mm cartridge in the chamber, he let the bolt go forward and flicked the selector switch to semiautomatic.

If he was forced to use the AK to take out the second man, he had to do it with the first shot. In the jungle, a single shot could mean almost anything. A burst of automatic fire, however, even a short burst, could only mean one thing, a firefight.

The other soldier on the team was getting agitated. His buddy had stepped off the trail to take a leak but hadn't caught up with him again. Impatiently calling his name, he hurried back down the trail toward Bolan's hiding place, the muzzle of the AK in his hands seeking a target.

Taking his time to get a good sight picture, the Executioner let the man get right on top of him before he squeezed the trigger, drilling a 7.62 mm round through the man's heart. His eyes went wide and without a sound he pitched forward on his face.

Bolan darted out of his hiding place, the muzzle of his AK zeroed on the soldier's head. The dull, sightless eyes told him that a second round wasn't needed.

When he reached down to drag the body off the trail, he saw the small two-way radio clipped to the straps of the man's chest pack. Holding the radio to his ear, he heard an excited burst of what he took to be Chinese. He could hear the question in the speaker's voice. Turning the radio off, he stuck it in the thigh pocket of his flight suit. Though he didn't speak the language, it might come in handy later.

As soon as the body was dragged back into the underbrush and the tracks erased, he kneeled beside the corpse and stripped off the chest-pack ammo-magazine carrier. Going through the pockets, he found a tin of Taiwanese canned fish and a rice-and-pork-fat ball wrapped in a banana leaf. Even traveling light without a rucksack, he had brought a snack.

Along with the mag carrier, the warrior also took the man's sun helmet. His flight suit was close in color to the uniforms the troops were wearing, and with the AK-47, magazine carrier and sun helmet, he should be able pass for one of them from a distance. But only from a distance. There was no way he could disguise his Caucasian height, his skin color or his blue eyes.

He had everything he needed now except a canteen. Neither of the two soldiers had been carrying one. But there were enough streams in the jungle to drink from until he could find something to use for a water container.

After adjusting the straps on the magazine carrier to fit his broad chest, Bolan slipped into it, put the sun helmet on his head and switched the AK over to safe. He knew that Kuhn Sa followed Mao's dictum—for a guerrilla force to survive, it must exist within the local population the way a fish lives in water. Since that was the case, he was going to go fishing.

Checking the position of the sun, he started out for the northeast. The Executioner was back in his element.

MAJOR LIM FROWNED as he listened to the radio report from the search party leader at the Harrier crash site. He had expected better things from the veteran sergeant he had put in charge. One of his two-man teams had disappeared into the jungle, and the suspected attacker had vanished. Even though he had no positive proof, he knew that the other American had survived the crash of the Harrier. While the man was loose in the jungle, though, he shouldn't be too much of a problem.

More than one Long Nose had ventured into the mountainous jungle, and few of them ever came out alive. This one would be no different. Kuhn Sa's eyes were everywhere. The man wouldn't escape. Sooner or later a villager or tribesman would send word of him, if the snakes and the tigers didn't get him first.

Lim briefly considered taking over the search for the American himself. It had been a long time since he had known the thrill of hunting a man through the jungle. Following the tracks and signs of a man who was running for his life was intoxicating. The uncertainty, the fatigue and the panic were so easy to see in the signs he left behind. Lim liked to wait patiently until he saw that the prey was on his last legs, then let him know that the hunters were close behind. That's when he really saw what his prey was made of.

Some men simply gave up and welcomed the death that was following them. Others got a renewed spurt of energy and tried to run even faster. Some, however, turned to fight like a cornered tiger. Those were the ones Lim enjoyed the most. He liked smelling a man's adrenaline over his rank sweat. He savored seeing the fear mixed with defiance in a man's eyes as he died.

Lim knew, however, that Kuhn Sa wouldn't let him lead the hunt this time. His assignment was to keep track of the Russian pilot and see that he was ready to fly the jet at all times. As far as the veteran Chinese jungle fighter was concerned, it was a low-level assignment and should have been given to a lesser man. He was the security chief for Kuhn Sa's holdings, but the drug lord had insisted that he see to it personally.

But the fact that he had been given the task was an indication of the great value Kuhn Sa placed on the mercenary pilot. Until the skies over the Golden Triangle were free of enemies, the Russian was vital to the security of the operation.

What would happen to Galan once the threat was ended was another matter entirely. Lim was already composing his request to be allowed to release him in the jungle so he could track him down. It wasn't that he had anything against the pilot, not at all. It was just that he had never tracked a Russian before.

That would be in the future, however. Right now he had to find the other American flier. As long as the man was loose in the jungle, Kuhn Sa's security wasn't assured.

He picked up his radio microphone and started calling his scattered units along the trails and passes leading both in and out of Kuhn Sa's sanctuary. No matter which way the American ran, he would be found.

8

Yuri Galan was overjoyed when he learned that one of the Americans from the downed Harrier had been captured and was being returned to the camp. He hoped that it was the pilot, the man he had bested in his first aerial combat. His English was rusty, but he wanted to talk to him.

He remembered reading that British, German and French pilots in World War I had been feasted in grand style by their captors before being sent off to confinement. He wanted to do the same for this man and ordered his women to prepare an extraspecial meal. He even broke into the following week's ration of vodka to make sure that the evening would be an unqualified success.

Major Lim hadn't been happy at first about Galan's request to meet the captive American, but he realized that it might not be a bad idea after all. He knew how effective the "good guy-bad guy" interrogation technique was, and he could use the Russian mercenary as his "good guy." He would let the Russian pilot play out his fantasy of aerial camaraderie and see if he could turn it to his advantage.

JACK GRIMALDI HAD BEEN in his cramped bamboo cage for only a couple of hours, but its charm had already worn thin. When the search team grabbed him in the jungle, he had been blindfolded before being hustled onto the chopper and flown away. When he arrived at wherever he was, the blindfold had stayed in place until he was dumped in the cage.

Since then, he had been left alone, but he knew that was standard procedure with captives. Supposedly, being left alone would drive home the reality of his capture and sap his will to resist. With him, however, this was time he could put to use trying to assess the damage he had done to his left leg. He had banged it while separating from the ejection seat, and it had stiffened.

Sitting on the packed-dirt floor of his cage was making matters worse, and it wasn't big enough for him to lie straight out and get comfortable. At least it was tall enough for him to stand erect. When the leg hurt him too much from sitting with it drawn up, he could stand for a while to rest it.

Since he hadn't heard another chopper land in the hours since he had been imprisoned, he assumed that his captors hadn't been able to run Bolan down. But that didn't surprise him. Even alone in the jungle, Mack Bolan wasn't an easy man to put your hands on. Most of those who tried drew back a bloody stub for their efforts. Knowing Bolan as he did, he knew that the warrior was coming for him. And no man was as good in the woods as he was, especially alone in hostile territory. All Grimaldi had to do was stay alive long enough to be rescued.

Even though the Executioner was known for performing miracles, he was going to have to watch himself when he got to this place. Grimaldi couldn't see much from his cage, but what he could see told him that he was being held at a major camp, not some outpost. There were more than a dozen fair-size buildings hidden under the trees—mess halls, barracks and everything else that went along with a military installation.

What he had heard, however, was more important than anything he had seen. On the flight, his captors had talked freely in what he thought was Chinese. He didn't speak the language, but he had heard a name that was well-known to anyone who fought in the international drug wars—Kuhn Sa. If Kuhn Sa was the drug lord behind the Freehand, he had a problem. He sure as hell wasn't looking forward to the interrogation he would get from him.

He looked up when he heard a helicopter approaching, but didn't think that it meant Bolan had been captured. He got to his feet anyway and tried to brush his flight suit clean. When he saw the group approaching his cage, he knew that his face-to-face meeting with the infamous Kuhn Sa was upon him. But for all the hundreds of pages he had read about the so-called lord of the Golden Triangle, none of them had prepared him for what he now saw.

Kuhn Sa looked like an elderly waiter in an upscale, big-town Chinese restaurant—until you looked into his eyes. There was power in his flinty black eyes, absolute power that could condemn hundreds to death without blinking.

The bodyguards with the drug lord were hard cases as well. They were trim, well-trained jungle warriors who had come up through a hard school. Unlike the swaggering, overarmed punks who usually surrounded Latin American and Mafia drug lords, these men had survived hard-fought battles against well-armed enemies to get where they were. Everyone from the Red Chinese to the CIA had tried to take control of the Triangle at one time or another. The fanatic Phatet Lao had come the closest, but even they had been turned back by the tortuous terrain and men who weren't afraid to die for their leader.

Standing beside Kuhn Sa was a tall, hatchet-faced man, wearing a fresh olive-drab uniform and an officer's pistol holstered on his belt. He spoke to the guards, and they opened the door to Grimaldi's cage and motioned for him to come out.

"My commander would like to know whom he is speaking to." the officer said in English.

"I'm Jack Grimaldi, and I'm a pilot for the American Drug Enforcement Administration."

The expression on Kuhn Sa's face didn't change when the reply was translated. He spoke briefly, then the interpreter turned back to face the pilot.

"Why did you fly over our territory, Mr. Grimaldi?"

"I was looking for that fancy Russian jet fighter you've got hiding out here."

"And what were you going to do when you found it?"

Grimaldi kept his voice flat. While he was going to tell the truth, he didn't want to sound flippant. "I was going to do my best to shoot it down."

"And why did you want to do that?"

The Stony Man pilot addressed his answer directly to Kuhn Sa. "That fighter has murdered the crews of four airplanes, and I wanted to put an end to it."

"I am not a murderer, Mr. Grimaldi," Kuhn Sa said in accented English. "I am just a businessman, nothing more."

Grimaldi was surprised to hear the drug lord speak such good English. But considering the scope of his drug empire, it was no surprise. English was the international language of commerce, even drug trafficking.

"This is some business you have here," Grimaldi stated.

"I merely produce a product that is in great demand," Kuhn Sa said modestly.

"And you are one of the richest men in the world because of it."

"Look around you." The drug lord spread his hands. "Do you see signs of great wealth here? This is not Hong Kong or even Singapore. My wealth is in my people and in the land that we hold against all invaders."

"Your business kills far too many people in my country."

"I am sorry for that," Kuhn Sa replied. "But I did not create the demand for heroin in the United States. I do not advertise it on your television, I do not put up billboards and I do not sponsor sporting events. Rather than attacking me, I suggest that you and your agency would be better advised to attack the reasons that so many Americans seem to prefer the oblivion of my drugs to living in the world's richest nation."

There was nothing the pilot could say to that. The drug lord had hit it right on, but that didn't excuse his making millions from the sufferings of others. He could call it a business all he liked, but it was still a deadly plague on civilization.

"There wouldn't be a demand for your poison," the pilot answered, "if it wasn't so readily available."

"I would not grow it if there was not the demand."

Again, Grimaldi could make no argument.

"What's going to happen to me now?" the pilot changed the subject. He didn't really want to know the answer to the question, but figured it would save him a lot of mental wear and tear.

"You will stay here as my guest."

"I don't get a bullet in the back of the head and a shallow grave? I thought that was the standard treatment around here."

"Like I said, Mr. Grimaldi, I am not a murderer."

There was nothing the American pilot could answer to that without putting his head in a noose, so he said nothing. The only intelligent thing he could do right now was stay alive and see if Bolan could get him out of this mess.

AFTER THE INTERVIEW, Grimaldi was surprised when he wasn't put back in his cell. Instead, he was taken to a small bamboo house hidden under the trees. A man was waiting in front of the open door. When he got closer, he saw that the man was another Caucasian.

"I am so glad to meet you," the man said as he walked forward, his hand out. "I am Yuri Galan. You are the American pilot, no?"

Grimaldi looked the Russian up and down. "Yes, I'm the pilot, Jack Grimaldi, and you're the bastard who shot me down, right?"

"I shoot you down, correct," Galan answered. "But I do not know that other word."

"Bastard?"

"Yes." Galan nodded. "That word."

Grimaldi kept a straight face. "It's an American slang word for a Russian pilot."

"Please come into my house, Jack Grimaldi. We have so much to talk about."

The Stony Man pilot doubted that, but there was no harm in seeing what the Russian was up to.

The main room in the house wasn't large, but it was comfortable by Asian standards. Rice-grass mats covered the floor, and there were several pieces of well-carved wood furniture. The two young women in native dress who stood against the far wall of the room also added to the comfort level. It wasn't a Moscow apartment, but he doubted the Russian was complaining.

Galan motioned to one of the women and she came forward with two glasses and a bottle on a lacquered tray.

"Vodka," Galan explained when the woman offered one of the glasses to Grimaldi.

The pilot took the glass. He really didn't care for vodka, but there was no point being a jerk about this. Plus, in this place he could really use a contact, even if the only candidate for the job was a mad Russian who was acting like this was a Snoopy and the Red Baron comic strip. He was better than nothing.

"Here's to you, Yuri." Grimaldi knocked the vodka back with an expert flip of his wrist.

Galan smiled broadly as he refilled the glass. "Here is to all Russian and American pilots."

"Right."

The Yak pilot downed his glass in one gulp, too.

"Come," he said, taking Grimaldi's arm. "I have prepared dinner for us."

Grimaldi followed. He was hungry and the Russian was sure to have better chow than they were serving in the local bamboo slammer. He would eat hearty and hope it lasted him a long time.

JIM RANSOM HAD A PROBLEM. Not only had his assistant been shredded by a rocket in the aborted attempt to interdict a heroin shipment and the Harrier been attacked in its hangar, but the two Washington special agents had also gone missing. Their jet was several hours overdue.

He probably should have called Washington an hour or two earlier, but since Grimaldi hadn't filed a flight plan, he'd had no return ETA to go on. He had waited until the Harrier should have run her fuel tanks dry, then he waited a little longer.

It wasn't going to be an easy call, and he wasn't looking forward to making it, but the time had come. He reluctantly reached for the secure phone on his desk and direct-dialed the DEA duty officer in headquarters. It took only a few moments for him to make his report. The duty officer asked no questions but told Ransom to stay where he was while the information was passed on to higher authority.

He was still sitting at his desk when the phone rang fifteen minutes later. When the Justice Department operator told him that Mr. Hal Brognola was on the line, he stiffened, waiting for the ax to fall on his neck. It had been a long time since he had been in Washington, but Hal Brognola was one name he hadn't forgotten. The last time he had heard, Brognola had been working organized crime, but that had been some time ago and things change.

"Jim Ransom?"

"Yes, sir."

"This is Hal Brognola. I understand you've got a problem in Thailand."

"Yes, sir, I'm afraid that I do."

"Talk to me."

Ransom was sweating with more than the heat when he finished with his brief rundown of the events of the past three days. There was a long pause on the other end of the satellite-link line.

"I'd say you definitely have a problem," Brognola finally said.

"What do you want me to do, sir?"

"Nothing. All I want you to do is to make a daily report. When Belasko and Grimaldi get back, they'll have further instructions for you. Until then, you are to do nothing."

"Yes, sir." Ransom couldn't keep the resignation from his voice. Doing nothing in this case meant that he wouldn't get a chance to salvage anything from the disaster. All he could do was try to hang on so he wouldn't lose his pension.

"And, Ransom?"

"Yes, sir."

"They'll be back."

"Yes, sir."

The station chief put the phone back on the cradle. The Golden Triangle had swallowed up better men than those two and hadn't even burped. Nonetheless, if Hal Brognola wanted to believe in the Tooth Fairy, who was he to explain the facts of life to him? He'd heard that things in D.C. had gotten too strange for words lately, and now he believed it.

9

When the sun started to sink behind the forested hills, the day sounds of the jungle faded and the Executioner stopped for a short break. He had been on the move constantly since leaving the site where Grimaldi had been captured and was ready to rest for a while. Plus, this was the time of day when it was smart to stop and rest.

For a man traveling alone in the jungle, dusk was the most dangerous time of day. The background sounds of the jungle were his first line of alert. Any change in the background noise level could be a sign of danger and dusk was when the day sounds ended and the night sounds began. He would start out again when darkness covered the land.

While he waited for the sun to drop behind the hills, he reached into his pocket for the food he had appropriated from the search team at his landing site—a tin of Taiwanese canned mackerel and a rice-and-pork-fat ball wrapped in a fresh banana leaf. For most Westerners, it wouldn't have been much of a meal. But he had eaten far worse too many times and was glad to have it.

After opening the tin with the point of his knife, he drank the vegetable oil the fish was packed in. Then he alternated between bites of the sticky rice ball and the salted fish. The fish would make him thirsty again, but he would have to ignore it until he came across another stream.

By the time he was done with his meager meal, the sun was all the way down and night was suddenly upon the jungle. Twilight didn't last long in the tropics. With the darkness came the sounds of the night dwellers, the mating calls mingled with the cries of the eaters and the eaten. Death was never far away in the jungle, but tonight the eaters of life had some serious competition.

Bolan waited a full thirty minutes before moving out again, letting his eyes completely adjust to the dark. This time he kept to the trails instead of trying to break brush. There were dangers that went with following the trails, but he could move faster on them. Plus, at night it was easier for him to hear other men on the trail. Not that he expected to run into anyone. Search teams couldn't read the signs to track him at night.

A mile or two farther on, a young male tiger waited beside the trail. The only sign that he was alive was the slow rise and fall of his sides as he breathed in the scents of the night. The smell of a man reached him, but this particular man didn't smell of fear or caution. Though hungry, the young tiger decided not to try to dine on this prey. With a low snarl, he slinked off, his belly low to the ground.

Bolan heard the tiger cough as he moved away from him through the underbrush. He thought tigers to be beautiful animals, but he was glad that this one had decided to leave him alone. He had enough on his plate right now without having to kill a hungry tiger.

JACK GRIMALDI WAS BEING very careful with the vodka Galan insisted that he drink in endless toasts. He blamed his abstinence on a bad stomach, and the Russian bought the story. He wasn't stinting on the food, however, and was packing as much of it away as he could. The roast pork and chicken with steamed vegetables, along with savory sauces and rice, were coming in a seemingly unending flow. Every time he emptied his bowl, one of the women filled it for him again.

"This is great food, Yuri," he said, holding his bowl out for more pork.

"Thank you," the Russian answered. "The girls are very good cooks. They make my life here very enjoyable. Is that the right word?"

Grimaldi could well believe that. He didn't know much about Russian women, but they would have to be something to compare with these two flowers of the Orient. Being a mercenary pilot for a drug lord paid well.

"That's the right word all right." He smiled at the woman filling his bowl. "Enjoyable."

He was feeling as much at peace with the world as a captive could when one of Kuhn Sa's troops appeared at the door. He said something to one of the women, who in turn spoke in Russian to Galan.

"I am sorry," Galan said in English, "but you have to go now. Someone is here who wants to talk to you."

"Who is that?"

"You will see," the Russian replied cryptically.

From the expression on Galan's face, Grimaldi knew that he wasn't going to like the next phase of the evening's program. He also knew that he had just been sucked into a "good guy-bad guy" routine, the interrogation technique known in the trade as "Mutt and Jeff." No sweat. At least he was aware of what was coming next.

The Russian pilot led him out to the porch, and he wasn't surprised to see Kuhn Sa's interpreter waiting for him with several guards. "I am Major Lim," the officer introduced himself. "And I need to ask you a few more questions about your mission."

"But I told Kuhn Sa all about it this morning," Grimaldi protested.

Lim looked him up and down. "I am not Kuhn Sa. My commander is too trusting sometimes, but I have more experience in dealing with men like you. You are not the first DEA man who has come up here."

Grimaldi didn't doubt that. "What more do you need to know from me?"

"I need to know where I can find the other man who was in the jet with you."

Grimaldi shrugged. "I didn't see him land, so I can't help you. We had trouble getting out of the Harrier. I wasn't in a good position when I punched out." He pointed at his leg. "I messed my leg up when the seat separated, and it was all I could do to get my parachute to deploy properly."

"You did not see him when you were in the air?"

"Yeah, I saw him, but he was quite far away from me, and I was having trouble with my parachute."

"So you said."

Lim waited before asking his next question. "You had a radio when you were captured. Did you try to contact him after you landed?"

"I tried, but the radio didn't work."

"So you do not know if he survived the landing?"

"Like I said, I was having trouble with my parachute and was too busy trying to save my own ass to worry about him." Grimaldi shrugged. "He's a big boy and he has to look out for himself."

"We will find him, you know."

Grimaldi remained silent.

After staring at him for several seconds, Lim spoke to the guards and Grimaldi was taken back to his cage.

MACK BOLAN ENCOUNTERED the first of the search teams right after dawn. Rather than try to sleep through the cold night of the high mountain jungle, he had kept on the move instead. Moving at night had its risks, but he had wanted to cover as much ground as he could while still fresh. The closer he got to his objective, the more cautious he would have to be.

Right before dawn, the warrior stopped and found a hiding place to take a short nap. Next to dusk, the most dangerous time in the jungle was the dawn. Again, it was the time when the background noises changed as the nighttime predators gave ground to the day hunters.

A short time later, he woke to the smell of coffee and saw that it was light. Smells traveled far on the chill, damp morning air of the jungle, particularly hot smells. What he smelled was someone boiling coffee, and the chances were good that that someone was from the opposition. The odor was coming from the northeast, wafting on the faint morning breeze. The smell was inviting, but it was an invitation to slaughter.

Glancing at his watch, the Executioner saw that he had slept for a little over an hour. It was time to get back to work. Getting to his feet, Bolan slipped into the jungle. Rather than bypass these men, he needed to see if they were a search team looking for him this far from the crash site. If that were the case, he would have to change his tactics.

It took him a half hour to make his way carefully to the source of the coffee smell. Parting the brush in front of him, he saw a small open space alongside of the trail he had been following. Three men wearing uniforms similar to those of the soldiers ferried to the Harrier crash site were sitting around a fire, eating their breakfast. The fire was small and smokeless, the kind that only veteran jungle troops made, and that alone was enough to identify them.

Although they were eating, their AKs were close by their sides, another sign that they were veteran troops. What the warrior didn't see was a radio, and that might make the difference. He could take them out, and no one would know that they had been killed until they failed to return to their patrol base.

If he were to continue moving fast, he needed their supplies, particularly their food and canteens. Despite cold nights and daytime humidity above ninety percent, a man could sweat over a gallon of water a day in this terrain. It had been twenty-four hours since he'd had the one long drink at the stream he'd passed. He needed a way to carry water, and their canteens would do nicely.

The Executioner didn't intend to give the members of the search team a chance to defend themselves. This was combat, not a stupid game. Aligning his AK's sights on the man facing him, he slowly took up the slack on the trigger.

The veteran jungle fighter's instincts had to have told him that he was in someone's sight picture. As soon as Bolan started to squeeze the trigger, the Thai flung himself sideways and shouted a warning.

When the warrior's first shot drilled through clean air, he thumbed the AK's selector switch to full-auto. So much for trying to do this the easy way.

A short burst took out one of the men who still had his back to him. By then, the man who had shouted the warning was bringing up his AK. Bolan rolled off to the side. A burst of gunfire cut through the brush where he had been lying, and he instantly got off a return volley.

Bolan's rounds stitched his opponent across the chest and spun him onto the small fire, where he knocked over the coffeepot.

The third hardman had been slow getting to his weapon. He hesitated as if trying to decide whether to fight or run. That hesitation cost him his life.

The Executioner snapped the AK into target acquisition and took out the enemy gunner with a long burst. The soldier still had a look of puzzled indecision on his face as the AK slugs punched through his lungs and heart.

When the echo of the last shot faded away, the warrior kept his position for a minute. When there was no movement from any of the three bodies, he stepped out, his Kalashnikov's muzzle covering them. A quick check revealed that they were dead. He rolled the one corpse off of the fire and quickly went about salvaging the equipment he needed for his march.

Rummaging through the three rucksacks, he took the food he found and transferred it to the one that fit him best. He removed the loaded magazines from their ammo carriers and the grenades from their pouches and put them in the rucksack, as well. Lastly he took four of their one liter Chinese plastic canteens, slinging two of them over his shoulder and putting the other two in his sack. Now he was ready.

Leaving the bodies where they lay, the warrior slipped back into the jungle. Before the day was out, the scavengers would find them and erase any traces of how they had died. The sun was coming up over the mountaintops, and it was going to be another fine day in the Golden Triangle.

MAJOR LIM WASN'T PLEASED with the outcome of the expanded search for the second American from the downed Harrier. He had more than two hundred troops spread out over three hundred square kilometers, and no one had seen a sign of him yet. If the evening report from the search teams was still negative, he would have to rethink this situation. The report of the three-man search team being wiped out this morning put the situation in a new light.

He knew that the team could have been ambushed by almost anyone. Kuhn Sa's troops weren't the only ones who used the Golden Triangle as a sanctuary. They weren't even the only ones growing poppy. Several Triads and countless tribes had staked out plots and were in the opium trade. Somehow, though, he didn't think they were responsible. But the two men who had disappeared from the crash site, and now these three, had been killed by someone.

While it was unlikely that a sole American airman would have taken on those three men by himself, that was what the evidence pointed to. Although the tigers and other scavengers had been at the bodies, they didn't rummage through the men's packs and take their canteens. As unlikely as it seemed, it was beginning to look like this American was coming north to try to rescue his companion.

Lim smiled. If that were the case, he welcomed him. Any Long Nose who ventured alone into the Golden Triangle was either a fool or a brave man, and the major hoped that it was the latter. It had been some time since he'd had a worthy opponent.

He shouted for his orderly. If the American was coming to him, he had to reposition his troops. Too many of them were guarding the trails, rivers and mountain passes leading south to the cities. Pulling them back would tighten the cordon and ensure the American didn't change his mind and slip away.

After the orders were given to pull his troops back, Lim went to have another talk with the captured pilot. Grimaldi had said that he thought that his back seat man had been hurt in the ejection. Obviously, however, he was well enough to take on a search team and kill them all.

Lim took two guards with him when he went to see the American. He wasn't afraid that the pilot would get away from him, but he wanted them with him as a sign of his status. He had learned that showing high status was helpful when dealing with prisoners. Also, the man had to be convinced that there was no way he was going to escape. Then the interrogation would bring fruit.

10

Major Lim made a point of checking on Jack Grimaldi early in the morning. Going from a comfortable dinner with the Russian pilot to spending the night in a cramped bamboo cage might have brought the reality of his situation home to him. One way or the other, though, Lim would learn everything the American knew before he was finished with him.

"Did you enjoy your breakfast, Mr. Grimaldi?" Lim asked his prisoner.

"I sure did, Major. It wasn't as good as the dinner your Russian pilot put together last night, but cockroaches and week-old rice has always been one of my favorite meals."

"You make jokes now, but I wonder how much longer you will do it. I don't think that it will be too much longer before you realize that you are never going to leave this place."

Grimaldi looked around the jungle and smiled. "How are the winters around here, anyway? I guess with the monsoon, you get a lot of rain."

Lim ignored the pilot's wisecracks. He had interrogated many men in his day and saw Grimaldi's remarks as false bravado, nothing more. He knew it wouldn't be long before the American ran out of smart remarks. That was when he would see what this man was made of.

"By the way," Lim said. "It appears that your companion was not hurt after all when he ejected from your jet."

Grimaldi kept his face from showing his emotion. "Why do you say that?"

"We have proof that he is alive and well."

Since the major was talking about Mack Bolan, that could only mean that someone else was dead and the body had been discovered. If Bolan had unexpectedly run into one of Lim's search teams, he would have had no choice but to leave their bodies behind. But then the Executioner had a habit of leaving bodies behind no matter where he went.

"You do not have a comment to make?" Lim looked surprised. "You are not happy that your comrade survived the crash?"

"I'm glad he's alive, sure." The pilot shrugged. "But I barely knew the dude, you know. It's not like we're roommates or anything. I'd never even met him before we were assigned to this mission."

Lim wasn't sure if he believed Grimaldi's nonchalant response, but for the moment, it really didn't matter. When he had the other American in a cage beside him, he would play them against each other. That was when he would see what these two men were made of. In the end, though, not even that would matter. Neither one would ever get out of the jungle alive.

"Before long," he predicted, "you will have a chance to get to know this man much better. There is no way he can escape my troops."

Grimaldi didn't bother pointing out that Bolan had escaped them so far and had apparently left bodies in his wake. He expected to see him again soon, but not as a prisoner. The next time he saw Mack Bolan, the warrior would be cutting him out of the cage.

"I hope he gets away, of course," Grimaldi said honestly. "But if he doesn't, at least I'll have someone to talk to."

Lim allowed a small smile to cross his face. "You'll be able to talk to him for a long time, Mr. Grimaldi. I promise you that."

With that, Lim turned and walked away.

BOLAN HID in the dense brush until the sound of the chopper rotors overhead faded away. For the second time that afternoon he'd been forced to hide from a passing helicopter, but he didn't mind. Both of them had been heading in the direction he was traveling. He had taken a big gamble when he set out to find Grimaldi, and he was glad to have his hunch confirmed.

He'd kept on the march all day covering at least another twenty miles, and was now deep inside enemy territory. The Golden Triangle was an ill-defined area of several thousand square miles of jungle-covered mountains and valleys. There were no towns and few villages, and those few were mostly populated by the mountain tribes who grew the opium poppy. The drug lords and the troops who controlled the region lived like an army in the field, constantly on the move.

Theoretically Grimaldi could be almost anywhere in this vast area. Bolan was betting, however, that he was being held at one of the larger semipermanent camps known to be in the jungle. All he had to do was find exactly which one.

Both of the choppers that had passed overhead had been flying at a fairly low altitude, which made him think that they had been on an approach to a landing zone at one of those camps somewhere to the northeast. It would be too easy if this particular helicopter LZ was also being used by the jump jet. But maybe the gods of war would be on his side this time. Considering how this mission had gone so far, it was about time he had a change of luck.

If he was close to a camp big enough to have a landing pad, though, he would have to be even more careful. A camp that important to the day operation would have security patrols working the jungle perimeter.

No sooner had that thought crossed his mind than he heard the sounds of troops coming down the trail toward him. The clink of metal on metal and the rattle of equipment was faint, but unmistakable.

He ducked back under cover and parted the foliage with the muzzle of his AK. A few minutes later, he caught a glimpse of a four-man patrol passing by. From their uniforms and equipment, they looked to be the same troops as the search parties he had run into earlier. By now he should have slipped past all the search teams looking for him, so this was confirmation that he was close to a base camp.

As soon as the troops were well past, he got to his feet and cautiously crossed over the trail. He hadn't come all this way to stumble into a patrol that wasn't even searching for him.

TWO HOURS LATER, Bolan reached what he hoped was his destination. At the end of a valley lying inside a horseshoe-shaped ridge was a large camp built back under the towering trees. He saw a cluster of bamboo buildings erected on ground cleared of underbrush, with people moving between them.

Keeping to the edge of the ridge, he worked his way around to the north side of the camp until he found a good observation point. The first thing he spotted was the Freehand VSTOL fighter hidden back in the trees under a large jungle-camouflage net. From above, it would have been difficult, if not impossible, to spot under the trees.

A small, irregularly shaped clearing had been cut out of the jungle in front of the jump jet to serve as both a helicopter landing pad and the fighter's launch point. Whoever had cut the clearing had been careful to leave the natural underbrush in place so it wouldn't appear from the air to be as man-made.

From the swarm of men servicing the Yak jet, this had to be the fighter's home base, not just some place where it landed between missions. That meant that the camp would be very well guarded. Kuhn Sa wasn't going to risk his prized jump jet to marauders.

It also meant that this was probably where Grimaldi had been taken. His captors would want to interrogate him to learn how the DEA planned to counter their new air-defense fighter.

The number of men, women and children walking around the bamboo buildings tucked under the trees also indicated that this was a major installation. Unlike a real military force, these troops had their families living with them in the field. Not that there was much danger for them. For better than a hundred miles in all directions, the hills and valleys were under the control of the drug lords and their private armies.

A hundred-mile radius beyond that was a buffer zone, a no-man's land, where even well armed government troops didn't care to enter too often. And when they did venture in, they came in strength and with gunship support. They also stayed just long enough to convince American politicians that they were actively doing something useful in the international war against the drug trade.

The Executioner was certain that he was at the right place. All he had to do now was figure out where Grimaldi was being held and get him out of there. He'd watch and wait.

THE SUN WAS LOW in the sky when Bolan heard shouts from the center of the camp. Looking out from his observation point, he saw two dozen troops fall out in front of the biggest building with their weapons slung over their shoulders. When they lined up in formation, he realized that they were the guard detail for the evening.

An officer marched out of the building to stand in front of the troops and gave them their orders for the night. When he returned to the building, two sergeants took command of their squads and marched them away. One of the twelve-man squads unslung their AKs and took up a tactical formation as they moved off into the jungle to the south of Bolan's position. The other squad went to the north.

He watched the two groups closely. As the night perimeter patrols, they were the ones he would have to deal with. He figured he could make his way into the camp and free Jack without being seen, but evading the roving patrols on the way out might be another matter, particularly if Grimaldi was hurt.

That problem could wait, however. Right now he had to get ready for his infiltration and that meant paring down the gear he was carrying. Shrugging out of the rucksack, he quickly sorted through its contents.

Two of the ChiCom stick grenades went into one of the side pockets of his flight suit. The extra AK mags went into the other pocket. Lastly he took one of the canteens, filled it all the way to the top so it wouldn't slosh and slung it over his shoulder.

When he had everything he thought he would need, he put what was left back into the rucksack and pushed it under the brush. He hated to leave it behind in case he wasn't able to get back to it. But if Grimaldi was hurt and had to be carried, he wouldn't need the extra weight.

Next, he removed the bolt cover of the AK and checked the action to make sure it was clean. An AK would fire dirtier than any other assault rifle he knew of, but a soldier with a dirty weapon just might lose his life because it misfired. When he was assured that the weapon would perform as expected, he checked the magazines. One of them proved to have a bent feed lip, so he removed the rounds and discarded it.

Even though he knew that his Desert Eagle was clean, he pulled it from his shoulder holster and checked it over. He then took one last look at the camp and curled up in his hiding place for a nap. The Executioner had learned a long time ago to get his sleep in the field whenever he had an opportunity. There was no point in trying to go in there until the camp was asleep so there was no reason for him to stay awake.

Setting his mental alarm clock for after midnight, he closed his eyes.

11

The jungle was dark when Bolan awakened. Glancing at his watch, he saw that it was a little after midnight, time to move out. Getting to his feet, he took a drink from one of the canteens he was leaving behind. Since he didn't have night-vision binoculars, he would have to get in closer to finish his surveillance of the camp. Regardless of what he had seen during the day, the camp would look different at night and he had to scope it out before he went in after Grimaldi.

A half hour later, he found a well concealed position barely twenty yards from the edge of the camp and halted for his last look-see. Several of the low bamboo buildings were lit with the soft yellow glow of kerosene lanterns, which was both good and bad. The light would make it easier for him to find Grimaldi, but he would have to be careful not to be backlighted.

There were also a few electric lights showing in what he took to be the headquarters building. The muted hum of a gasoline generator told of power being produced to run them and the communications equipment. The noise, though, was a plus. It would help mask his movements.

After watching the camp for more than an hour, Bolan was ready to make his move. He had watched long enough to have a feeling for the locations of the buildings and the routine of the interior guard. He still hadn't located Grimaldi, however, and would have to do it the hard way.

BOLAN HAD NO TROUBLE infiltrating the camp. It was slow going, though. Even as late as it was, there were quite a few people moving around and he had to keep to the shadows. As he had expected, the biggest problem was discovering where Grimaldi was being held.

The first buildings he checked were barracks or family quarters for the married troops. A couple of windowless buildings with padlocks on the doors that he took for warehouses weren't likely to be used for holding a prisoner.

Behind the fifty-man mess hall with the charcoal fires from the evening meal still smoldering, he saw a small bamboo cage standing alone in an open area. There was a dark, huddled shape in the bottom of the cage that had to be his friend.

A sentry suddenly appeared from behind the tree next to the cage as the Executioner was about to leave cover. In the glow from a nearby lantern, Bolan saw that his AK was slung over his shoulder and he was buttoning his fly. He froze in the shadows and watched to see if the man had been posted to watch over Grimaldi's cage.

When the sentry continued on his way, the warrior moved out in a crouch. Halting in the shadows a few yards away, he called out softly, "Jack!"

The Stony Man pilot awakened instantly. But since he didn't know who might be watching, he didn't move. "Is that you, Sarge?" he whispered.

A shadow detached itself from the darkness and silently moved up to the bamboo cage. "Can you walk?" Bolan whispered.

"I banged my leg when I punched out, but I'll crawl if I have to. Just get me the hell out of here."

"Stay down," Bolan cautioned as he drew the chisel-pointed Tanto knife from his boot sheath. Crouching beside the two-inch-thick bamboo bars that made up the cage, he reached down to the ropes binding the poles together. The knife's razor-sharp edge slid through the nylon ropes as if they were string. He only loosened the poles at the bottom so they could be pulled back into place and, at a sentry's cursory glance, would appear to be intact.

Once the poles were cut free, he slowly pulled them apart, creating a man-size gap at the bottom. Grimaldi squeezed through and crouched on the ground beside his rescuer. "Glad you could finally make it to the party. What kept you?"

"I had to walk. The bus wasn't running."

After pulling the bamboo bars back into place, Bolan handed Grimaldi his AK and an extra magazine. Drawing his Desert Eagle from his shoulder rig, he flicked it off safe. "Let's go."

THE EXFILTRATION WENT almost as smoothly as Bolan's penetration. A couple of times they had to freeze when someone walked by, and once they rolled under the stilts of one of the bamboo houses to allow a family with several sleepy kids to slowly meander past.

When the two men reached the last building and were headed for the jungle, Grimaldi reached out for Bolan's arm. "We better come up with a plan to knock out that Yak. We can't leave it behind."

"How about emptying a magazine into a strategic spot in the jet engine or the nose cone?"

The pilot shook his head. "That's not going to be good enough. They might be able to get the parts to repair it. We have to blow it up."

Blowing up the plane would be like poking a stick into a hornet's nest, but Bolan knew they had to try to do it. The primary mission was to take out the fighter, and since they had failed to do it from the air, they might as well try to do it on the ground. Until the renegade Russian jump jet was turned into junk, it would be a danger to everyone who was fighting to stem the flow of drugs from the Golden Triangle.

"Do you know where their armory is?" Bolan asked.

Other than the two ChiCom-style stick grenades in the side pockets of his flight suit, he had nothing in the line of high explosives to use on the Yak. If he could find a satchel charge or even some blocks of plastic explosive, he could make a bomb big enough to destroy the aircraft.

"I haven't the slightest. Why?"

"I don't have any explosives with me, only two ChiCom stick grenades," Bolan answered. "You think they'll do enough damage that they can't repair it?"

"They should work okay if we can put them in the right place. Which means we'll have to get in close. Do you know where it is?"

"It's parked under the trees on the other side of the clearing," Bolan answered. "I'll show you.

WHEN THEY GOT CLOSER to their objective, Bolan saw that Kuhn Sa was taking no chances with his prized Russian VSTOL fighter. He could see at least four guards posted around the camouflaged aircraft. And if there were four men on duty, at least four more guards would be available for their relief somewhere close by. There would also be a sergeant of the guard and probably a radioman or a runner. That was too many people to take out silently

"How many troops does this guy have in the area?" Bolan asked Grimaldi.

"I don't know. But I've seen several dozen, at least a company, if not more."

That was a lot of well-trained opposition for two men to overcome, so taking out the jet would have to be a stealth job. At least it would start out that way. There was no way the Executioner could figure the near-impossible odds of their coming out of this undetected. Since he had no way to detonate the grenades remotely, they would have to get right up to the aircraft, place the grenades, activate the fuzes and run.

"Can we throw the grenades and do the job?" Bolan asked.

"I don't think so. But I've got an idea. Why don't I try to just walk up to it like the Russian pilot would?"

"Jack, you're crazy."

"Think about it," the pilot urged. "I'm wearing a pilot's flight suit, and to those guys, all us Round Eyes look alike."

"You're asking to get yourself killed."

"As long as we're here," he insisted, "we've got to try to take that fighter out."

Bolan had to agree with him. "Okay, let's do it."

Taking the grenades from his pocket, the Executioner unscrewed the metal caps from the ends of the handles to expose the pull rings for the friction fuzes. "Pull the igniter and you have four to five seconds to get clear."

"Got it," Grimaldi said as he put the grenades in the side pockets of his flight suit with the ends of the wooden handles within easy reach.

Bolan took up a good firing position at the base of one of the trees towering over the jet. Holding his Desert Eagle in a two-handed Weaver combat stance, he got ready to cover Grimaldi's move. "Go for it."

"I'll be back in a flash."

The pilot walked out into the clearing, his AK slung over his shoulder and the handles of the ChiCom grenades sticking out of his side pockets. He had walked only a few yards before a sentry stepped out from the shadows, his AK held at port arms across his chest.

Grimaldi approached the sentry, pointed to the Yak, then back to himself.

The sentry then barked something at him in clear Russian. When Grimaldi shrugged, the sentry snapped the AK down to cover him and shouted what Bolan knew to be an order for him to halt.

The Executioner's carefully aimed shot took the sentry in the chest. The big .44 slug spun him as it tore through his chest and dropped him on his face.

"Forget the plane!" he shouted to Grimaldi. "Run for it!"

Rather than immediately turn and run, the pilot snatched the grenades from his side pockets. Pulling the friction fuzes on both grenades, he threw the bombs as far as he could in the direction of the Yak. They both fell short and exploded harmlessly. Whirling, Grimaldi raced back to Bolan's location.

A second sentry raised his AK to fire at the fleeing figure. Bolan snapped two quick shots at him. Both of the rounds connected on target, and the sentry crumpled to the ground.

An AK on full-auto sounded from the warrior's left front. The burst passed over his head and struck a tree, sending wood splinters into his face. Even well-trained troops tended to fire high at night. Lowering his sights, he fired two more quick rounds. A high-pitched scream told him that at least one round had connected.

Grimaldi skidded to a stop beside him. Turning, he fired a long burst at his pursuers and dropped down to change the magazine. By now, the entire camp was in an uproar. Whistles shrieked, men shouted and lanterns were being lit in almost every building.

Bolan fired four more shots at fleeting targets. "Follow me," he said, dropping the empty magazine from the butt of the pistol. "I know the way out of here."

Fortunately the Yak was parked at the edge of the camp and the two men didn't have far to go before reaching the cover of the jungle. Once out of the direct line of fire, they raced to put distance between themselves and their enemies.

MAJOR LIM AWAKENED instantly with the first burst of fire, yelling for the duty sergeant as he scrambled for his uniform.

The sergeant appeared instantly. "Yes, Major?"

"Check on the American pilot!" Lim snapped.

"At once."

The sergeant spun to follow Lim's orders, but the Chinese officer knew without being told what he would find. The second American had somehow found the camp and had rescued his comrade.

Lim realized that he had seriously underestimated these two DEA men. He had taken Grimaldi's wisecracks as being false bravado, but he had been wrong. Now he knew that the mouthy American had been laughing at him. The pilot had known all along that his companion was coming for him and had just been biding his time.

He had underestimated the Americans, but he wouldn't make the same mistake again. And when he had his hands on those two men, they would seriously regret having made him look foolish. Thoughts of what he would do to them almost banished the anger he felt building, so he forced them down. The time for pleasure would come later. Right now, he had business to take care of.

Not stopping to lace up his combat boots, he dashed into his radio room. They might have pulled off the rescue, but he had them now. There was no way they could make their escape. He had two hundred troops to call on, and they covered the surrounding territory like a spider web.

Snatching the microphone from the radio operator's hand, he barked orders to his perimeter patrol units. Half of them he pulled in closer to the camp. Khun Sa wouldn't like to think that his expensive jet fighter hadn't been properly guarded. The remaining units he sent farther out, to preplanned ambush points along the trails leading to the south.

When his troops had their orders, Lim pulled the 9 mm Makarov pistol from his holster and racked back on the slide to chamber a round. He was going out to question the night guards to learn why the American had been able to infiltrate the camp and free the prisoner.

He anticipated that the sergeant of the guard would have to pay for this lapse of security with his life. Lim didn't mind losing the veteran, however. It had been so long since the troops had done anything more than patrol empty jungle that they had gotten slack. The sergeant's execution would serve as a good lesson to all of them.

The duty sergeant rushed back into the headquarters. "The American—" he began.

"I know," Lim interjected. "He is gone."

The duty sergeant couldn't understand why the major had a slight smile on his face as he rested his hand on the butt of his Makarov. "Tell the sergeant of the guard to report to me immediately."

"At once, Major."

12

As soon as Bolan and Grimaldi were several hundred yards into the jungle, the warrior halted their head-long run and pulled the pilot under cover with him. The only good thing about their situation was that the commotion at the camp had alerted the roving patrols. Bolan could hear them shouting to one another as they left their ambush positions to respond to the alert.

"Why are we stopping now?" Grimaldi hissed. "We've got to get out of here!"

Bolan leaned over to bring his mouth close to the pilot's ear. "I want to give the ambush teams time to respond to the alert and start moving in toward the camp. They're easier to spot when they're on the move."

Grimaldi nodded his understanding. Now that Bolan was there, he was glad to let him run the show. He'd had his time in the woods, too, but grunt warfare in the jungle was the Executioner's specialty, and he was welcome to it. The Stony Man pilot was truly at home only when he was behind the controls of an aircraft.

Bolan didn't even think of trying to go back for the rucksack he had stashed in his earlier hiding place. The area was close to a rendezvous point for the roving patrols of perimeter guards, and it was crawling with troops. They would have to make their getaway with what they had with them—the AK, the Desert Eagle, the remaining ammunition for the weapons and one canteen.

It wasn't much, but he had been in the jungle before with less and it would have to do. Plus, there was always the chance of picking up more equipment the same way he had gotten what little they had.

Behind them, they heard the shouts from the aroused camp and saw lights moving around. It would take the drug lord's troops several minutes to discover that they weren't hiding somewhere in the camp. And in those precious minutes, they had to get enough of a head start that they could outrun the pursuit that was sure to come. It should be enough time, but it was going to be tight.

A couple of minutes later, Bolan got to his feet and slowly scanned the area. While the camp was still in an uproar, the area around them was quiet. As he had thought, the roving patrols had been sucked in close to the camp, leaving holes in the perimeter. All he had to do was find one of those holes, and they would be gone.

"Okay," he whispered, tapping Grimaldi on the shoulder, "let's go."

The warrior took the lead. Picking up one of the major trails leading south away from the camp, he headed out at a slow run. This was the direction the opposition would expect them to go—southwest to-

ward the plains. He would leave an obvious trail for
them to follow. Farther on, he would break their trail,
backtrack and then head out in another direction. It
would take them longer doing it that way, but it would
be much safer.

Favoring his leg, Grimaldi followed Bolan into the
darkness.

YURI GALAN WAS DREAMING when the first shots
sounded. In his deep sleep, his mind turned the shots
into a dream of his being back on the pistol range at the
Red air force academy. The explosions of the two grenades, however, snapped him back to the camp in the
jungle. When another burst of AK fire sounded, he
jumped out of bed.

Fumbling in the darkness, he slipped into the fatigue uniform and boots he had been issued. Only now
did he miss the weapon that he hadn't been issued.
Major Lim had told him that he would have no need
for a weapon as long as he stayed close to the camp.

Lim hadn't said anything about the camp coming
under attack. However this situation turned out tonight, in the morning he would make sure that he
found a gun even if he had to go to Kuhn Sa himself to
get it. He had signed on to fly the Yak, not to be a target on the ground.

Galan walked out onto his porch, making sure that
he didn't make any fast moves. As the only Caucasian
in the camp, he didn't want anyone firing at him by
mistake. For all the noise and shouting, there was little to see. Several small groups of men were running

around with flashlights and lanterns, checking the buildings. Squads of Lim's troops were forming up and quickly moving out into the jungle.

His women soon joined him and stood inside the door, talking quietly. That was the biggest problem with not speaking the language. Most of the time, he didn't have the slightest idea what in the hell was going on.

BOLAN AND GRIMALDI HAD WALKED less than a half mile when the warrior heard a low voice speaking into a radio. They had left the noise of the camp behind, and sound traveled far on the cool air of the high mountain jungle. They could stay ahead of men on foot, but there was no way they could outrun a radio transmission.

Motioning for Grimaldi to lay low and wait, Bolan started forward to recon the enemy position. If they had reached an ambush point, he would try to bypass it. If it was just a look-out post with a couple of men, however, he might take them out before moving on. Even two fewer pursuers might make a big difference later on.

Moving to the side of the trail they had been following, the Executioner crept forward until he was even with the voice on the radio. Two men stood beside the trail, but they were too close together to be an ambush team. Unless there were more men waiting in ambush in front of them.

Bolan walked parallel to the trail back toward where he had left Grimaldi, and found a third man waiting in ambush. He had been posted only twenty yards down the trail from the two with the radio. But in jungle as thick as this, he might as well have been on the other side of the moon for all the good his two teammates would be to him. The warrior decided to start with him.

The lone man was alert, but with Bolan coming at him from the direction of his two teammates, he didn't react to the slight sounds coming from behind him. Too late, he turned his head. But the Executioner was on him, his hand clamping the man's mouth and the Tanto knife stabbing for his throat.

The blade entered the side of his neck and drove all the way through his windpipe, severing both the jugular vein and carotid artery. His feet kicked briefly before the sudden loss of blood shut down his brain.

Bolan reached down, picked up the man's AK and quietly snapped out the folding bayonet. He also flicked the selector switch up to the safe position. By now, the troops looking for them had to have entered the jungle, so he had to do this without risking a shot. He also picked up the dead man's sun helmet and placed it on his head. The helmet and the AK in his hands would get him close enough to the other two to go to work.

He stepped out onto the trail and walked back toward the ambush position with his head down. The team leader saw him coming and stepped out to meet him rather than calling out. When he got within two arm lengths, Bolan snapped the AK toward his enemy and lunged just as he had been taught so many years ago on the bayonet range in basic training.

The triangular spike bayonet plunged into the man's neck right under his chin. Bolan's thrust drove it through the soft tissue of his throat and up into the brain stem at the base of his skull.

Bringing the AK back toward him, the warrior grabbed the corpse by the back of his magazine carrier and held him erect as he withdrew the bayonet. Looking over his shoulder, he saw that the radioman was sitting by the radio and had a set of earphones on his head. Unfortunately for him, he hadn't heard his comrade die.

Bolan carefully lowered the corpse to the ground and stepped forward just as the radio operator looked up and recognized the danger. He tried to get to his feet, but the steel butt of the AK smashed him between the eyes.

He turned as he fell, presenting his back to Bolan. A quick thrust buried the bayonet in his kidney. The shock choked off his cry, turning it into a gasp. A twist of the blade opened an artery and quickly bled him internally.

Hearing a noise behind him, Bolan spun to find that Grimaldi had joined him. "Thought you might be having trouble," he explained.

"No trouble," Bolan said as he knelt to pat the bodies down. He discovered a couple of grenades on the second body and stuck them in his pockets.

Suddenly the radio came alive again. "Someone's being called," Grimaldi said, holding the earphones to his head and hearing a call sign being repeated in Chinese. "And it's probably these guys."

Bolan folded the bayonet back on his AK and slung the assault rifle over his shoulder. "We'd better get going before they send someone to see why they're not answering."

LIM'S RADIOMAN TURNED to him. "Patrol Sixteen doesn't answer, Major," he said hesitantly. The major didn't like bad news under any circumstances, but he was in an especially vile mood tonight.

Lim realized that there could be any number of reasons why they didn't answer, but he wasn't about to underestimate the Americans again. "Who's in charge of that unit and where are they supposed to be?"

"Corporal Chin's their leader, Major, and they were posted at the first ring on the Bo Pao Trail."

Lim went to the map and located Patrol Sixteen's position. His orders had sent the troops to positions along all the trails leading out of the camp. The positions were in two rings surrounding the camp, so that if the fugitives broke through the first ring, he could move people in from the second ring to contain them.

The major took an AK from the rack on he wall. "Tell the mobile team to meet me at the start of the Bo Pao Trail on the edge of the camp. I'm going to investigate this one myself."

"At once, Major."

Lim was grimly amused when the sergeant in charge of the mobile team wouldn't meet his eyes. Word of the execution of the guard sergeant who had allowed the Americans' escape was having its intended effect. Things had been too quiet in the Golden Triangle lately, and the troops had gotten soft. That would soon be a thing of the past, however. If the Americans managed to slip out of the rings, more executions would follow. Kuhn Sa paid his troops well, but he expected to get his money's worth.

"I need to go to the first ring position on the trail," he told the NCO. "Patrol Sixteen was stationed there, and they do not respond."

"At once, Major."

Lim let the sergeant take the lead as the team set off slowly down the trail. He was anxious to reach Patrol Sixteen's location, but he wasn't going to risk running into an ambush. A half hour later, Lim halted when the sergeant held his hand up. The patrol went to ground while the sergeant went forward alone.

A few minutes later he came back. "They are dead, Major. All three of them."

"Let me see this."

When Lim examined the bodies in the beam of his flashlight, the signs were clear. Whoever had taken out these men had done a professional job. One man had had his throat cut not with a slice, but with a thrust. Another had been bayoneted, taking the point directly up under the chin and into the base of the skull. The third man had died from a bayonet thrust to the kidneys.

These were the hallmarks of a man experienced in killing, and it fleetingly crossed Lim's mind that he was dealing with a warrior here. But he instantly dismissed that thought. The two Americans were DEA man, not warriors. The DEA was an overrated police force more suited to chasing street dealers and shuffling papers than to fighting in the jungle.

He did know, though, that quite a few DEA agents had had military service before they joined the agency, and that had to be the case with these two. The killing techniques they used were military. Nonetheless, their military training would soon be put to the ultimate test. His troops were probably the best jungle fighters in the world, and they were on home territory.

The Americans could run for a while longer, but there was no place they could go in the Golden Triangle where he couldn't find them.

"Give me the microphone," he ordered the radioman. "Now I know where they are going."

GRIMALDI WAS HAVING trouble keeping up with Bolan. A day and a half in the cramped cage hadn't done his leg any good, and it was protesting.

"Mack," he said, "I'm sorry, but I've got to stop for a minute. My leg's cramping up."

Bolan pulled off the trail and found good cover in the underbrush. "Sit down and hold your leg out," he told Grimaldi. "I'll try to massage the cramp out."

The pilot sat with his back against a tree trunk and extended his leg. "Before I forget," he said as Bolan's hands worked at his knotted muscles, "I need to fill you in on what we're dealing with back there."

"What's that?"

"To start with, Kuhn Sa's the one who brought that Yak down here."

The Executioner wasn't surprised to hear that. Kuhn Sa's financial empire could well afford the millions the experimental Russian fighter must have cost him.

"And I actually got to meet him. He flew in after I got captured."

"What did he want?"

"He wanted to know why we were trying to shoot down his jump jet. He gave me the 'I'm just a businessman trying to make an honest dollar' routine. I told him that I was just following orders, and he gave me a lecture on the evils of American society.

"The weirdest thing, though, is the guy who's flying the Yak. He's a Russian named Yuri Galan and is ex-Red air force. Apparently when Kuhn Sa bought the jet, he came as part of the deal. I met him, too, when he pulled some kind of Snoopy and the Red Baron number and invited me to dinner last night and talked about fighter pilots being the 'knights of the air.'

"The guy in charge of the camp calls himself Major Lim and I think he's Chinese. Whatever he is, though, he's a proper bastard, as McCarter would say. I'm glad you got me out of there before he began working on me. He was starting with the Mutt and Jeff routine, but I could tell he was anxious to try out his new set of thumbscrews."

"Try the leg now," Bolan suggested, reaching down to help Grimaldi to his feet.

The pilot carefully stood and flexed the leg. "Thanks. It's a lot better now. I think I can keep going."

"You sure?"

"I'm sure that I don't want those bastards catching up with me."

"I'll take the point," Bolan said, "and try not to run away from you. In fact, I think it's time that we broke this trail and did a little evading. We've come far enough that we can backtrack and try to throw them off the trail."

13

The next morning, Yuri Galan was angry. After all he had done for the American pilot, for him to have tried to destroy the Yak was unthinkable. He had also learned that the English word "bastard" wasn't really an American slang word for a Russian pilot. The American had made a fool out of him, and Galan didn't like that.

The last laugh, however, would be on the American and whoever had taken him out of the camp. It had been a daring rescue, to be sure, but they had a long way to go before they would be safe. And from what he had seen of Kuhn Sa's operation so far, there was no place in Asia where they could run without being found.

Major Lim had more than two hundred troops searching for them on the ground. In addition, three helicopters were crisscrossing the treetops, with squads inside ready to exploit any sighting. Lim was satisfied with the coverage, but as far as Galan was concerned, it wasn't enough. He was going to join in the search himself. He hadn't bothered to talk to the major about it. He was just going to do it.

Walking out to where his VSTOL fighter was parked, the Russian pilot saw the blast marks on the jungle floor where the two hand grenades had exploded. When he thought of what they would have done to his plane, he got angry all over again. He expected that kind of behavior from an uncivilized guerrilla fighter, not from a fellow fighter pilot.

He was glad to see that Lim had placed extra guards on the Yak this morning. Had they been there last night, his plane wouldn't have been endangered. The jet was more than simply his meal ticket in Southeast Asia, it was his life. If the fighter was destroyed, he would be of no further use to these people. And from what he had seen so far, useless people didn't live long in the jungle.

Pulling his helmet down over his head, he climbed into the cockpit, strapped in and motioned for the crew chief to start the turbine. As soon as all the instruments were in the green and the jet engines were warmed up, he signaled for the ground crew to push the fighter into the clearing.

Galan felt his adrenaline start to pump when the Yak cleared the treetops and he transitioned to level flight. He was on the hunt again, and he liked how it felt. The Yak wasn't equipped with the sensor devices that the Harrier carried, but Galan was an experienced ground-attack pilot and knew what to look for from the air. With his eyes added to the helicopters and ground-search teams, the Americans were as good as dead.

At least they would be dead if he spotted them. He knew that Lim wanted them taken alive for question-

ing, but if he saw them, he would fire. If Kuhn Sa
didn't like it, he could always blame the language bar-
rier. He would swear that he had heard Lim say that he
wanted them dead.

BOLAN AND GRIMALDI KEPT stock-still until the sound
of the Yak fighter had faded into the distance. For the
second time that morning they had gone to ground at
the sound of Galan's jump jet making a slow, low-level
pass over the jungle. Even so, they both knew there was
little chance of the Russian spotting them.

A more dangerous sound would have been the wop-
wopping of rotors. The helicopters carried more than
one set of eyes and could get lower to look through the
thick canopy over their heads. For some reason,
though, they had managed to keep out of the search
patterns of the choppers.

"We could sure use a couple of Stingers right about
now," Grimaldi said, referring to the American-made,
shoulder-fired antiaircraft missiles.

"We're just going to have to keep under cover
whenever he flies past," Bolan replied.

"We do too much of that, and the ground teams will
catch up with us."

"Not if we can keep ahead of them." Bolan glanced
down at the pilot's leg. "If you can."

Grimaldi smiled thinly. "I really don't have a lot of
choice, do I? Major Lim isn't going to be happy that
you pulled me out of there. He had big plans for the
both of us, but he was waiting until his boys rounded
you up before he got started."

"Forget about him," Bolan said, stepping out into the open. "We've got a jungle to worry about. Let's get going."

Though burdened with only the AK, Grimaldi was having trouble keeping up with the pace Bolan set, but it couldn't be helped. In an escape and evasion situation, the first day was critical. If they could get through the first twenty-four hours, their chances of pulling it off increased greatly.

A half hour later, they came to another ridge that had to be climbed. A hundred yards short of the top, Grimaldi's leg gave out again. "I've got to take another break, Mack," he said, his voice showing the strain he was feeling.

Bolan took a quick look around the jungle. This was as good a place as any to stop. He handed the pilot the canteen and pulled a ChiCom stick grenade from his side pocket. "I'm going back down to the flat," he said, "to leave the opposition a little reminder of life in the jungle."

The warrior walked several hundred yards back down the trail and picked a spot where the track was narrowed from the thick vegetation encroaching on each side. Stepping back into the jungle, he looked around until he found some young hanging vines. Taking the Tanto knife from his boot sheath, he cut two twelve-foot lengths of the thin, ropelike vine.

Off to the side of the trail, he unscrewed the metal cap from the end of the grenade's wooden handle, reached into the compartment and pulled out the pull ring on the end of the friction fuze cord. If he'd had a roll of issue trip wire, he would have simply tied the fuze pull ball to the almost invisible wire and ran it across the trail. In the dim light under the trees, the wire would go unnoticed.

Since he had no trip wire, he split the end of the vine, slipped the fuze cord into the cut, wrapped it around once and wedged it back in. Using a smaller piece of the thin vine, he tied the explosive head of the grenade to the base of the tree trunk.

Once the grenade body was tied securely in place, he trailed the length of vine with the fuze ball tied to it across the trail, positioning it at an angle, back the way they had come. Stretching the vine straight across the trail would have looked artificial. Running it at an angle looked more like nature had placed it there.

When he finished tying down the vine, he walked back a few paces and examined his booby trap. The vine looked natural, but he unbent a couple of leaves it had folded. A sharp eye could spot them as signs of an ambush. He also brushed away his boot prints before leaving.

If their pursuers tripped the vine and activated the grenade, they probably wouldn't take enough casualties to make any difference. What the grenade would do, though, was make them aware of the danger of booby traps, which would slow them. And with Grimaldi's injured leg, they needed all the help they could get.

Grimaldi looked a little better when Bolan got back. "You ready to go?"

The pilot grimaced as he rose to his feet. "Let's do it."

"How bad is it, and I want the truth."

"I'll be okay," he said, "just as long as I don't stop and let it get too cold."

The ghost of a smile crossed Bolan's face. "I don't think we'll have to worry about that."

"That's not really what I wanted to hear."

"We'll stop early tonight, though."

LESS THAN AN HOUR LATER, they were forced to stop again. The trail they were following broke out over the top of a ridge and led down into a valley.

Bolan called a halt behind the ridge and left Grimaldi there while he went forward to check out the valley below. There was a fair-size village where he might be able to steal food and supplies. But there was also a dark green helicopter parked at the village's northern edge. Lim's men had leapfrogged ahead of them to set up blocking positions.

But when the Executioner saw that the chopper's rotor blades were tied down, he got an idea. Had the aircraft just flown in for a brief stop, the blades wouldn't have been tied down. More than likely, it was temporarily being based out of the small village to transport the search teams looking for them. And if that were the case, it would still be there tonight.

"I think I've found your ride home," Bolan said when he got back to where Grimaldi was resting.

"What are you talking about?" the pilot asked, frowning.

"Come on up here," he said, extending his hand to help the pilot to his feet. "I want to show you something."

At the top of the ridge, Bolan pointed to the helicopter. "That's a Huey parked down there."

Grimaldi pulled himself up to get a better look. "Yeah, it's an old Charlie model. Probably left over from the war."

"And you can fly that thing in your sleep, right?"

The pilot looked at Bolan and slowly shook his head. "Mack, there's got to be a couple dozen soldiers down there. There's no way we can just walk in and take that chopper without their noticing what we're doing. And just what did you mean by *my* ride. You're not thinking of staying behind, are you?"

Bolan glanced back to the north, his jaw set. "There's still the Freehand."

"You can't take it out by yourself."

"As you said, we can't leave it and walk away," the warrior stated. "As long as it's up there, it's a danger to anyone who flies over the area. Plus, don't forget that Kuhn Sa's using it to haul heroin."

"So," Grimaldi conceded, "what's the plan?"

Bolan settled back into the underbrush and made himself comfortable. "First we get some sleep. Then when it's dark, we'll go down there. I'll draw the troops off to the south while you get in the chopper, take off and fly it back to Nakhon Phanom."

"Just like that?"

"Just like that."

The pilot shook his head. "Old pal, you've lost it. I can't leave you behind like that."

"You don't have much choice," Bolan said bluntly. "You're having trouble keeping up with me, and if we run into a patrol we can't handle, you can't run. Also, if I don't create a diversion to pull the troops off, you'll never get to that chopper and get it airborne."

Grimaldi didn't like it, but Bolan's assessment of their situation was right on, as always. Like it or not, he was holding them back.

"Plus," Bolan added, "one of us has to get the information about that jump jet back to Hal before they move it somewhere else. He might be able to get permission to put an air strike together if he knows where it is."

"Okay, okay," Grimaldi said. "You've convinced me. But how about if I pick you up on my way out?"

The warrior shook his head. "It's too dangerous. Your only hope is to crank up that helicopter and get the hell out of there as fast as you can. There's going to be a lot of lead flying down there, and if you stop for me, you'll pick up some of it."

Grimaldi saw the wisdom of that, too. As much as he might not like it, Bolan was right again. The most important part of the operation was destroying that Russian jet. He had been in the business long enough to know that the mission objective always came first. And, so far, their mission was uncompleted.

Grimaldi bowed to the pragmatism of the war he and Bolan knew only too well. "You're right," he said.

"One of us has to get back and I'm the pilot. But I'll come back for you. You can take that to the bank."

Bolan laid his hand on his friend's shoulder. "Let's just take it one step at a time, Jack. We have to get you out of here first."

YURI GALAN WAS DISGUSTED when he returned to the landing zone at the camp. He had spent most of the day in the air, and he hadn't seen a thing. He had badly underestimated the difficulties of spotting a man in the jungle. It had been completely different when he had chased rebels through the forests of Georgia. At least there he had been able to see the ground under the trees.

As he climbed down from his cockpit, he wasn't surprised to see Major Lim waiting for him. It had been stupid for him to take off without telling the man what he was doing. Lim was paranoid enough, even on a good day, and this wasn't a good day.

"You did not see a thing, did you?" Lim stated.

Galan shook his head. "No, Major. The jungle is much too thick."

"Now do you see why I did not ask you to join in the search?"

"Yes, Major."

"Before you decide to fly anywhere again, Galan, you will get my permission first. Do you understand?"

"Yes, Major, I understand."

"Good." Lim's face was expressionless. "General Kuhn Sa will be glad to hear that."

Galan heard the threat implicit in the Chinese officer's statement, but he didn't respond. He was too tired and much too frustrated to argue the point with him. But he would be more careful in the future.

14

Bolan awakened just as the sun was sinking behind the hills. When he looked over, he saw that Grimaldi was still sleeping. With his bad leg, the pilot had exhausted himself on the run from the camp and badly needed the rest. The Executioner was careful not to wake him as he made his way back up to the vantage point overlooking the village.

Small groups of soldiers were moving into the village from the south and west, probably patrols that were coming back from daytime search. Since the troops were congregating around the big hut in the center of the village, more than likely it had been taken over as their command post. That was SOP in most of these cases. The villagers would give the invaders the best of everything, hoping troops wouldn't destroy what little else they had.

Were it not for the villagers having to deal with the drug lord's troops on the one hand and the government troops on the other, they would have been able to live an almost idyllic life in the lush valley. As it was, every time they turned around, they had to share their meager goods with either one side or the other. The warrior had seen it happen in every war zone he had ever visited.

He also knew that he and Grimaldi were about to bring more grief to these people, but it couldn't be helped. The pilot couldn't keep up the pace, and Bolan couldn't abandon him. The good thing was that after the Stony Man pilot flew off in the chopper, the troops would think that they had both left the area and would leave the villagers alone again.

When he backed down from the ridge line, he found Grimaldi awake.

"What does it look like now?" the pilot asked.

"The chopper's still down there."

"So you still want to go through with it?"

Bolan nodded. "I don't see that we have much choice, do you?"

"You got a plan?"

Bolan smoothed the ground in front of him and picked up a small stick for a pointer. "Here's how it looks to me," he said. "I'm going to work my way around to the south and get set up. While I'm doing that, I want you to..."

GRIMALDI CARRIED the AK-47 at port arms, his thumb on the selector switch and his finger resting on the trigger. Bolan had given him the assault rifle because he knew that he'd be able to get another one before the night was over. Plus, if the pilot had to fight his way out, he would need all the firepower he could get.

Along with the 30-round magazine in the assault rifle, he had four more mags stuffed into the side pockets of his flight suit. The additional hundred and fifty 7.62 mm rounds should see him safely through the night. If they weren't enough, the plan wasn't going to work and they would both die.

Grimaldi made it all the way down to the Huey unseen. He'd taken cover behind a rice dike when two soldiers walked past, but hadn't run into any guards watching the chopper. Now that he had reached his objective, he crouched under the tail boom for one last look around.

Bolan had seen that the main rotor had been tied down so it wouldn't move around in the wind and put stress on the rotor-head bearings. Rather than risk damaging the rotor by trying to run it up while it was tied down, Grimaldi had to release it first. He found the nylon tie-down cord and pulled on it gently to bring the end of the flexible rotor blade down far enough that he could unclip it.

When Grimaldi released the blade, it creaked loudly as it sprang back up, and he froze. When the noise didn't bring a reaction, he got to his feet. The moon wasn't up, but the faint reflection of the kerosene lanterns in the village cast enough light that he didn't have to feel his way up the side of the chopper's fuselage.

He missed seeing the man's combat boots sticking out of the open side door of the troop compartment until he almost stumbled into them. Jumping back, he dropped to the ground, his AK at the ready.

He hadn't seen a sentry guarding the Huey because the man who should have been watching it was sleeping inside the troop compartment. The way the man was lying, Grimaldi couldn't reach him without possibly waking him up. And he sure as hell couldn't risk a shot.

He slowly unfolded the short spike bayonet from under the barrel of his AK. Swinging it forward on its pivot, he quietly slid the lock ring over the assault rifle's muzzle. It clicked into place with a barely audible snap. It had been a long time since basic training, but he still remembered what the drill sergeant taught him about using a bayonet. Thrust like you're trying to hit a target behind your man.

The reflected light from the village didn't illuminate the inside of the troop compartment and he couldn't see the man's upper body clearly. But he knew where his chest had to be. Holding the AK at high port, he stabbed down as if he were trying to drive the bayonet through the floor plates.

The chisel-pointed bayonet slid up under the guard's chin. His feet drummed on the aluminum floor plates for a moment, then he was still.

Wrenching the bayonet free, Grimaldi wiped the blade on the guard's uniform, unsnapped it and folded it back under the barrel. Grabbing the corpse by the feet, he dragged it out and laid it under the belly of the helicopter between the skids.

He glanced down at his watch and saw that most of the hour Bolan had allotted him to get ready was gone. The Executioner would be making his play soon and he had to be prepared. Climbing up into the right-hand seat of the chopper, he closed the cockpit door behind him. The Huey had standard military seats, and he slid the armored side of the seat forward to protect at least some of his body.

He didn't dare risk turning on the red cockpit lights, but his hands hadn't forgotten the locations of a Huey's controls. He had spent more time in the right-hand seat of the Bell choppers than most people had behind the wheels of their family cars. His right hand automatically fell to the collective control stick beside his seat and his finger rested on the turbine's starting trigger.

"Come on, Mack!" he muttered under his breath. "Let's get the show on the road!"

ON THE OTHER SIDE of the village, Bolan prepared to go to war. During his recon, he had spotted several of the perimeter guards and knew where they had emplaced one of their machine guns. That gun's open-topped, sandbagged bunker would be his opening gambit. Taking the machine gun out would immensely improve both his and Grimaldi's chances of survival. Plus he intended to turn the weapon against his enemies.

As he had expected, the bunker was occupied by only two men. As an added bonus, one of them was asleep. Kuhn Sa's troops were experienced jungle fighters, but obviously they weren't taking the threat of two American fliers seriously.

As silent as a shadow, he worked his way behind the soldier standing guard beside the machine gun. Reaching out, he clamped his hand over the man's mouth, jerked his head to one side and slashed the

Tanto knife across his enemy's throat. Held erect in Bolan's arms, he bled to death in a few short seconds.

The Executioner lowered the body to the ground and stepped over to the sleeping man. Clamping his hand over his mouth, he drove the chisel point of the knife deep into his heart. The man's eyes flashed open, but dulled almost instantly in death.

Two down.

He took the chest-pack ammo-mag carrier from the first body, quickly adjusted the straps to fit his chest and slipped his arms into it. Taking up the man's AK, he checked to make sure that there was a round in the chamber, then flicked the selector switch to safe.

As the warrior settled behind the RPD machine gun, he spotted an RPG-7 launcher with a round in place lying against the inside of the bunker. That would come in handy later.

He aimed the machine gun in the direction of the perimeter positions closest to him and held down the trigger. Glowing green 7.62 mm tracers swept across the rice dikes as the 500-round, linked-ammo belt ran through the receiver of the gun.

When the end of the ammo belt ran dry, Bolan abandoned the weapon. Snatching up his newly acquired AK and the RPG-7 launcher, he rolled out of the bunker. Scattered AK fire slammed into the sandbags behind him.

Now it was up to Grimaldi.

WHEN THE FIRST BURST of machine-gun fire broke the silence of the night, Grimaldi waited. Bolan had warned him not to be in too big a hurry to crank up. He did, however, start running through the prestart checklist.

As his hands moved over the controls and switches, he recited the checklist under his breath. "Battery, on. Inverter switch, off. RPM warning light, on. Fuel, main and start, on. RPM governor, decrease. Throttle, flight idle." Reaching down with his right hand to the collective control stick, he twisted the throttle open to flight idle.

He rested his finger on the starting trigger and waited. "Come on, Mack," he muttered. "Give me a signal."

The flash of an exploding grenade turned into a fireball as stacked fuel cans for the chopper went up in flame. Grimaldi took that as his signal and he pulled the start trigger on the collective. The electrical starter whined, and the big Lycoming T-33 turbine in the rear of the Huey burst into life with a screeching roar. Above his head, the forty-eight foot, two-bladed main rotor slowly began to turn.

As the turbine rpm built and the rotor blades slowly picked up speed, he released the start trigger. Holding the throttle at the idle position, he quickly checked the instruments to make sure that everything was in the green. When he realized that the faint glow from the lights in the instrument faces was outlining him in the cockpit, he shut them off. He didn't need to see the instrument readings to fly this aircraft.

WHEN BOLAN HEARD the whine of the Huey's turbine cranking up, he raised the RPG-7 launcher to his shoulder. It was time to raise the ante to keep everyone's attention on him, not Grimaldi.

Lining the launcher's sights on the command post, he pulled the trigger. The rocket's prop charge boosted the round out of the launcher with a whoosh and the flash of the back blast. A few yards out the main rocket motor cut in and sent the 85 mm antitank rocket screaming for the bamboo hut.

He had purposely aimed low, and the rocket impacted at the base of the wall. The bamboo didn't have enough resistance to detonate the rocket's warhead, but the packed earth floor inside did. The explosion blew burning thatch and bamboo in all directions. In seconds several buildings were on fire.

IN THE LIGHTS from the fires, Grimaldi saw troops running toward him. As he watched, one man stopped, raised his AK and fired a burst at the Huey. He heard one of the rounds punch through the chopper's skin and instinctively ducked. His main rotor rpm were still too low for a textbook takeoff, but he was flat out of time. The next burst could easily sweep the cockpit.

Ever so gently he pulled up on the collective control to feed pitch to the rotor blades. Without looking at the tachometer, he felt the blades slow their building revolutions as they bit into the cool night air. The cold turbine was already screaming at full throttle, so there was no use trying to twist the throttle grip past the stop.

He flattened the pitch just a hair to let the blades accelerate faster.

When the pilot heard the welcome *wop-wop* sound of the two-bladed rotor coming up to speed, he knew that the blades were spinning fast enough to lift him off the ground. He pulled more collective, and the Huey staggered into the air like a three-legged dog trying to chase a rabbit. Once free of ground effect, he nudged forward on the cyclic control in his left hand. The Huey's tail came up, and he started to move forward.

Grimaldi kept the chopper's nose low as he flew through a storm of AK fire. It made him an easier target, but it let him pick up airspeed faster than if he tried to climb out of the range of fire before he was flying fast enough.

A bullet smashed through the Plexiglas of the cockpit door and stopped against the seat's side armor. Another round punched through the cover under the pedals and clipped the sole of his combat boot. He heard other rounds drill through the chopper's thin aluminum skin behind him. As long as they missed the hydraulics and electricals, he'd be okay. He'd flown Hueys that looked like Swiss cheese before.

When he finally had almost a hundred miles per hour airspeed showing on the dial, he hauled all the way up on the collective. The Huey leaped into the sky like a homesick angel. Looking over his right shoulder, he saw a good-size firefight raging in the village.

Glowing green tracer fire crisscrossed the paddies. The flare of an RPG back blast briefly lit up the center of the village. The resulting detonation of the rocket flared against one of the rice dikes. His impulse was to go back down and do everything he possibly could to help his old friend, but he immediately checked that thought. He knew that whatever he did would only make the situation worse. The Executioner had chosen his fight, and Grimaldi had to run from it this time.

Bolan had given him his orders, and he would follow them, but he would be back.

BOLAN HEARD THE HUEY fly away. It was time for him to disengage and get out of there. Slamming a fresh magazine into the bottom of the AK, he headed back up the ridge. When he reached the top, he looked back and saw that the villagers had gotten the fires under control. He hoped that none of them had gotten caught up in the cross fire, but he knew that was a vain hope. War, even the never-ending war against drug lords, always brought death to the innocent, as well as the guilty.

Using the stars to guide him, he set his course for the northeast and his unfinished business with a Russian Yak-141B jump jet.

15

The sun was just breaking over the Nakhon Phanom air base when the dark green Huey came in low and fast over the end of the main runway. Dropping down to waist level, it headed straight for the hangar where the Harrier had been readied for its fateful flight. The survivors of the Marine security detachment at the hangar thought nothing of the chopper landing until they saw that it was heading straight for them. Then they scrambled for their weapons.

At the last possible moment, Grimaldi flared out and brought the Huey in for a hot landing, its skids scraping on the tarmac. As soon as the chopper skidded to a halt, Marines ducked under the still-spinning rotors and stormed the cockpit.

"Hey!" Grimaldi shouted when he saw the M-16 muzzles pointed at him. "Don't shoot! It's Jack Grimaldi!"

"Get your ass out of the chopper, mister," a Marine sergeant shouted back, his M-16 muzzle unwavering. The pilot, who needed a shave and was wearing a filthy flying suit, didn't look like anyone he'd ever seen before.

Wincing as he stepped down to the ground, Grimaldi made sure that both of his hands remained in plain sight. "Get your sergeant or your captain out here ASAP," he ordered. "They know who I am."

"Just keep your hands up, mister."

Gunnery Sergeant Minery ran out of the hangar with Jim Ransom on his heels. The DEA station chief had been staying at the DEA flight operations office at the air base since the Harrier had gone missing. Hal Brognola had predicted that the two special agents would return, and he hadn't wanted to get on the wrong side of him again by not being on hand if they did somehow appear.

Ransom took one look at the pilot, then looked back at the Huey for Belasko. The dark-haired agent wasn't in the chopper. "Where's Belasko?"

Grimaldi shook his head. "He stayed behind so I could steal the chopper."

"You're kidding!"

Grimaldi's face was grim. "I never joke about things like that."

"Damn," Ransom said softly.

Brognola had promised that the two special agents would be back. He had figured it for a long shot at best, but had never thought it would happen like this.

"What happened to you?"

"Before I talk about that," Grimaldi replied. "I need something to eat and drink." He took a step and remembered his leg. "Then I need to see a doctor."

BOLAN GREETED the morning sun by pulling back off the trail he had been following to find a place to sleep for a couple of hours. He had kept on the move all night and figured that he had covered at least fifteen miles. So far, there had been no signs of pursuit, and if anyone tried to look for his trail now, he was too far away for them to catch.

Now that Grimaldi was safely away, he could concentrate on the mission at hand as soon as he got some rest. As much as he valued his long friendship with the pilot, he was glad to be alone. He always did his best work when he was on his own, even when he was in a jungle with no backup, very little equipment and an army surrounding him. Now he could go completely into his jungle-fighter mode.

The Executioner hoped that the opposition would think that he, too, had escaped in the stolen chopper. But he knew the danger of underestimating them. Whoever was running the show for the drug lord wouldn't be a fool. As soon as he had a chance to go over the reports from the survivors in the village, it would become apparent that someone had remained on the ground when the Huey flew away. And since the chopper hadn't been seen coming back for him, it would be realized that he had been left behind.

As soon as that conclusion was reached, the dogs would be after him again. But Bolan had no intention of hanging around for them. The opposition would be covering the trails and rivers leading to the cities to the south and wouldn't be expecting him to venture back into their stronghold.

But he had business to take care of, and since that business was deep in the Golden Triangle, he was going back.

As soon as he was rested, he would continue working his way back up to Kuhn Sa's camp to conclude his mission.

MAJOR LIM WASN'T HAVING a good day. Kuhn Sa hadn't been happy to learn that the two Americans had escaped, and had been even less happy about the means they used to escape. While the drug lord had more money in the bank than most small nations have in their treasuries, purchasing aircraft was always a long, involved process and cost far more than it should. The helicopters were vital to their operation, and the stolen machine would have to be replaced quickly.

Lim still had his head on his shoulders only because he had faithfully served Kuhn Sa for so many years, which allowed him to be forgiven this lapse. But his faithful service wouldn't excuse a second such mistake. Kuhn Sa's new orders were for him to have the two Americans hunted down and killed before they had a chance to fly out of Thailand.

This second task was proving to be even more difficult than finding them in the jungle the first time. But Lim's people were watching the airport in Bangkok and had shoot-to-kill orders, and he was confident that they would carry them out even against impossible odds. As with the eight men who had tried to destroy the Harrier in its hangar, the men at the airport would willingly die rather than fail.

The problem was that there was more than one way for the two Americans to fly out of Thailand. Since the DEA worked so closely with the Thai armed forces, there was also the chance of their flying out on a military aircraft. He could cover that avenue as well, but it was more difficult and it came at a higher price.

Recruiting men for his urban army of thugs and spies was easy. His agents looked for smart young men who wanted to live a life of adventure, and good pay. Finding men to infiltrate the Thai armed forces, however, was an entirely different matter. Most of his agents in the military had been recruited from men already in the Thai army and air force. These men, who were dissatisfied with their lot in life, and particularly their low government pay, had listened to his recruiters.

But few had actually signed up to live this life, which would bring execution if they were found out. Lim hated to lose any of these agents. They could cover the Thai military air bases, true, but he risked compromising them when they did. The agent who spotted the two men and made the kill would, of course, be lost. But Kuhn Sa had left him no choice. His orders were specific, and Lim was to spare nothing and no one to carry them out.

He thought briefly about moving the Yak fighter to a new location, but quickly put that out of his mind. Too much work had gone into creating the supply base for the fighter to just pick up everything and leave now. It had taken a great effort to gather the fuel supplies and support equipment the fighter needed. Moving everything would put the jump jet out of action for several days, if not weeks, while a new base was being cut out of the jungle.

It made sense to move the aircraft to a location that wasn't known to the two Americans, but that was a decision Kuhn Sa would have to make himself. The Russian fighter was his toy. He had come up with the idea to buy it, and he expected great things from it. So far, it had been useful, even Lim admitted that. But he wasn't sure if it was going to stay that way for much longer.

Kuhn Sa's operation had been so successful because it was spread over a vast area of jungle and almost impossible to pinpoint. Now, too much had been gathered at one place just to support the Yak, and more was on the way. A second warehouse to store heroin until it could be flown out was already under construction, and this made Lim nervous. Centralizing their operation made them vulnerable, and he didn't like the feeling.

GRIMALDI FLEXED HIS LEG as if expecting pain, but there was little. The doctor had given him a cortisone injection and wrapped the leg in an elastic bandage. It wasn't a hundred percent yet, but it would do if all he had to use it for was to fly a helicopter.

"Thanks, Doc. I think it'll be okay now."

The American doctor from the missionary school was used to patching up CIA and DEA men for everything from gun battles to whorehouse brawls. He didn't even bother asking how this guy had wrenched his leg. He knew he'd be lied to.

"You should keep off of it as much as you can for the next week."

"I'll try."

As soon as one of the Marines escorted the doctor back outside the hangar, Ransom asked, "What's your plan?"

"I'm going back after my partner."

"How are you going to do that?"

The pilot jerked his thumb toward the Huey sitting on the tarmac.

"Oh, shit."

"Let's go take a look at my ride."

Out on the tarmac, Grimaldi inspected the Huey carefully. Beyond the few bullet holes in the skin and the canopy, the ship looked to be in pretty good shape. He should be able to have it serviced and be on his way back to the Golden Triangle in minimum time.

When Captain Dave Jenson walked over, Grimaldi told him that he wanted the chopper towed inside the hangar out of the way of prying eyes. Then he wanted it gone over from top to bottom and readied for flight.

"How good are your contacts with the Thai air force people?" Grimaldi asked Ransom as he watched the Marine mechanics hook up his Huey to the towing tractor and fit the ground-handling wheels to the skids.

"Why?" Ransom wanted to know.

"I need a gunship armament pack for that thing, and I need it ASAP."

"I've never asked my contact for anything like that," the station chief replied. "I don't know if he'll be able to help you."

"There's always a first time for everything. And I need it yesterday. Belasko's out there and I'm going to need the firepower when I go back for him."

Ransom thought for a moment. "Okay," he said. "Get in my Jeep and we'll drive over to see him."

16

Jim Ransom's Thai air force contact turned out to be the base supply officer and the man was very glad to see the DEA station chief. The American was the source of most of his supplemental income, which almost every Thai expected to take in from the drug-trafficking wars.

"Mr. Ransom," he said, a broad smile on his face. "I have not seen you in some time now. How are you?"

"This is Special Agent Jack Grimaldi," Ransom said, getting right to the point. "He needs your help."

"Mr. Grimaldi—" the Thai officer bowed slightly "—I am honored to meet you. How may I be of assistance to you?"

"I need a complete gunship armament package for a C-model Huey."

From the look on the Thai's face, one would have thought the pilot had asked for the Buddha's head. "That may be difficult," he said. "We do not use that model UH-1 for gunships any longer, and the armament sets were disposed of a long time ago."

"How about a couple of 2.75-inch rocket pods, then? They're the same for the late models."

The Thai consulted a computer printout. "I have two of those on hand, never issued and still in the crates."

"Good. I'll take them."

The Thai looked at Ransom, who nodded his head.

"Since you don't have C-model minigun mounts, how about the universal fifty mounts?"

"I think that I may have some of those." The supply officer reached for a different computer printout. "I will have to look. It has been a long time since the Thai air force has used them, as well."

Consulting yet another printout, the Thai smiled. "I do have some of the universal mounts."

"Do they have the electrical firing connections that go with them?"

"I believe so."

"I'll need two of those as well as the weapons to go with them and the trigger solenoids."

Ransom again nodded when the Thai looked his way.

"This is not a purchase," the supply officer said as his clerk handed over the paperwork for the transaction. "I will have to have these weapons and mounts back at the end of your operation."

"You'll get them back," Ransom promised.

"The ammunition, though, will be billed as always. I do have to account for its expenditure."

"Of course."

"When can you deliver it?" Grimaldi asked.

"Probably early tomorrow," he replied with a shrug. "It takes a while to process the paperwork."

"Add a surcharge," Ransom said, "to speed things up."

"Certainly." The Thai smiled.

"What do you have to pay that guy to get that kind of cooperation?" Grimaldi asked as they were driving away with a Thai air force trailer packed full of weapons and gun mounts hitched to the back of the DEA Jeep.

"It's not all under-the-table," Ransom explained. "He's on the payroll as a foreign contractor for aircraft-maintenance support."

"Nice part-time job."

"This will cost us extra because he knows that we need it." Ransom shrugged. "It's highway robbery, but it's just the way business is done around here. If you want to play, you have to pay."

Grimaldi was no stranger to that system, but the Thais seemed to have developed it into a fine art. Usually, though, the military wasn't so blatant about it. Nonetheless, he had what he wanted and could go about his business while the DEA picked up the tab.

NOT ONLY WAS the Thai supply officer on the DEA payroll, he also worked for Kuhn Sa's network. He had been told to be on the lookout for the stolen helicopter and the man flying it. The payment he expected for that information would be even bigger when he reported that the pilot was arming the ship. In fact, it should be big enough that he would be able to buy that Toyota truck he had been looking at.

The information about the armament for the Huey was on its way to Kuhn Sa before night fell.

THE REPORT THAT Grimaldi's stolen Huey was being fitted with armament rocked Major Lim. He had told his agents in Nakhon Phanom to be on the lookout for the stolen ship, but he had never expected to hear that it was being armed. That could only mean one thing—rather than running back to the United States, the American pilot was coming back to the jungle to try to destroy the Yak one more time. And if that was the case, he had to talk to Galan.

Lim's duty runner found the Russian supervising the men working on his jump jet. The pilot didn't understand the urgency, but quickly followed him back to Lim's headquarters.

"What is the problem, Major?"

The Chinese officer briefly reported the information that had been sent from Nakhon Phanom, but Galan had trouble understanding the report. No matter what kind of armament had been fitted to the Huey, there was no way that the helicopter could take him out in a dogfight.

He had read about the famous incident where an American Cobra gunship had downed a Cambodian MiG-17 in the Vietnam War, and he knew that the Israelis had also claimed air-to-air chopper kills against jet fighters. But those had been combats against conventional jet fighters, not jump jets, and certainly not against a Yak-141B, the most maneuverable jump jet of all-time.

The report didn't make sense unless Grimaldi planned to attack him on the ground. If that was the case, he was in trouble. Beyond the radioed reports of Kuhn Sa's agents in Nakhon Phanom, Galan had no early-warning system to allow him to get his Yak into the air in time to defend himself.

He hadn't counted on something like this when he signed up to fly the VSTOL fighter for Kuhn Sa. His job was to use his jet to deliver heroin to the network of drug couriers. He had expected that he might have to use his talents to evade aerial patrols and maybe even go up against fighters during his drug-running missions. But he hadn't signed on to be a sitting target on the ground for a madman in an armed helicopter.

"If he is doing this," he told Lim, "you have to protect me and my plane. I will need a warning that he is coming."

"I am surprised at you, Galan. I would have thought that you had more courage."

"It's not being a coward to want early warning of someone who's trying to kill me."

Lim's thin mouth sneered at the Russian pilot's unmanly concerns. "Certainly your expensive Russian fighter is capable of dealing with an American helicopter that is at least twenty years old?"

"To deal with that Yankee's helicopter, as you put it," Galan snapped, "requires that I be warned that it is coming. I cannot keep my plane in the air twenty-four hours a day."

He leaned over Lim's desk. "That twenty-year-old helicopter can also destroy this camp while it is trying to destroy me and my fighter. If you will remember, it was the Americans who invented ground-attack armament for helicopters. I think it would be best for both of us if I have ample warning that it is coming.''

''That is a good point,'' Lim admitted reluctantly. ''I will see that you have your warning. But you had better make good use of it. If Grimaldi attacks this camp, Kuhn Sa will not be happy with you.''

''If you give me adequate warning,'' Galan said hotly, ''I will be ready to defend both myself and the camp.''

''That is what you are paid to do, isn't it?''

JACK GRIMALDI WAS LOADING his borrowed Huey for bear. The helicopter was being decked out with an armament package that the Bell factory had never intended the chopper to carry.

Even though he had originally asked for it, he knew that the standard Huey ground-attack armament package would have been of little use to him in an aerial encounter with the Russian jump jet. The standard load of 2.75-inch rocket pods and a 7.62 mm minigun was short ranged and wouldn't have carried the punch he needed against an opponent armed with 30 mm cannons and heat-seeking missiles. If he had to face Galan in the air again, he wanted something with much more range and power. Finding the old 50-caliber heavy machine-gun mounts had been a piece of good luck for a change.

Prior to installing the 7.62 mm miniguns on Huey gunships, the big fifties had been experimentally mounted as chopper armament. But the fifties hadn't been replaced because they weren't first-class guns. They were the best heavy machine gun that had ever been built.

In World War II, the big guns had been fitted to aircraft and had shot the best of the German and Japanese air forces out of the skies of Europe and the Pacific. Even in the early days of the jet age, the old fifty caliber had been standard fighter armament. And if they had been good enough to take out North Korean MiG-15s, they would work on a Yak-141.

Captain Jenson and his Marine mechanics willingly pitched in to help. Grimaldi had taken the Marine officer into his confidence, and when he heard the story of the pilot's missing teammate, he offered his men and their expertise.

Their tough inspection of the Huey had turned up a couple of things Grimaldi had missed on his initial cursory inspection. For one, an AK bullet had clipped one of the tail-rotor-control hydraulic lines. The leak was small, but it had almost drained the fluid from the critical system on the flight back. Before he could fly the machine again, it had to be replaced and the system purged.

The holes in the aluminum skin and Plexiglas were being patched with "hundred-mile-an-hour" tape, the combat aircraft mechanic's best friend. The main rotor blades also had a couple of AK holes in them. They were being patched with epoxy putty and sanded smooth.

While the Marines were servicing the turbine and airframe, Grimaldi was busy bolting on his makeshift armament package. Fortunately the stolen chopper was an ex-military gunship, not one of the look-alike versions originally made for the civilian market. Because of that, it still had all the electrical hookups for the weapons it had once carried. Otherwise there would have been no way for him to install a weapons-system wiring harness.

They were almost ready.

17

Mack Bolan was really in his element now. Earlier that morning he had come across a burned-out camp fire alongside a trail. After checking to find that the fire was long cold, he scooped up a double handful of ashes and charcoal and put it in the side pocket of his flight suit. Then he stopped to retrieve an empty fish tin with remnants of oil coating the bottom.

After ducking back into the jungle, he mixed the oil with the ashes from the fire to make a paste. When the mixture was the proper consistency, he applied it to his face and hands, turning them a dark gray. The warrior wiped the remainder of the paste on the front of his flight suit.

It wasn't the same as wearing real combat cosmetics and a camouflage uniform, but it was all he had for what he had in mind. Rather than simply waiting to stumble across Kuhn Sa's troops, he was going to actively hunt them down. That meant ambushing the trails, shooting up their campsites and otherwise striking when and where they least expected it.

The Executioner had been born in a guerrilla war, and he had learned the hard lessons of jungle warfare well. This time, though, he would be playing the role of the guerrilla fighter. *He'd* be doing the ambushing.

Bolan had spent most of the previous night keeping watch along a well-used trail in hopes of putting his campaign into operation. But when midnight came and he still hadn't made contact, he moved out to find a secure location to sleep for a couple hours.

Now he moved out again. Within a half klick, he caught the smell of wood smoke. Following his nose, he discovered a six-man patrol camp at a site on the side of a ridge. Two of the men were on guard—one tended a small fire—while the other four slept. It was a perfect setup for him to begin his guerrilla campaign.

The second sentry was on guard at the base of the ridge well beyond the small circle of light thrown by the fire. He was so busy watching the approaches to the high ground that he wasn't keeping an eye to the rear.

Slipping through the scrub brush above him, Bolan slowly worked his way up behind the sentry. The man had been alert, but he had assumed that the slight noises behind him were coming from his comrades in the camp. That assumption proved to be fatal. Too late he sensed something and spun, only to meet Bolan's attack.

Clamping his hand over the sentry's mouth, the warrior jerked his head up and to the side, exposing his neck. Once more, the Tanto knife made short work of a man's life. The razor-sharp blade slashed across the throat, severing the veins, arteries and tendons. Only the resistance of the man's spinal column kept him from being completely decapitated.

Bolan laid the body on the ground and patted it down. He found four ChiCom stick grenades and put two of them in his side pockets. The warrior had a more immediate use for the other two and unscrewed the metal caps on the ends of their handles.

Pulling the igniter rings to start the fuzes burning, he held the grenades for a second to let the fuzes burn down before lobbing the bombs high into the air over the sleeping camp. The detonations sounded loud in the night and the brief flashes of the explosions showed that they were on target.

Unslinging his AK, the Executioner unloaded a full 30-round magazine of 7.62 mm rounds into the confusion. The man tending the fire collected much of the long burst and went facefirst into the fire. The stench of burning hair and flesh smelled strong on the cool mountain air.

One of the sleepers rolled over to his AK and fired from a prone position, but the rounds went wild. Bolan aimed and sent a short burst to put him down. Firing from the hip, he swept the sleeping positions, but the man farthest away from the fire leapt to his feet and fled into the jungle without even stopping to grab his rifle.

The Executioner let the man get away unharmed. For the campaign he was waging, a survivor was worth much more than merely another casualty. When the man returned to his unit, he would tell of the sudden death that had come out of the night. The other soldiers would be even more cautious when they were in the woods the next time, and excessive caution on the part of the enemy made the warrior's job easier.

MAJOR LIM HAD difficulty believing the reports that kept flowing in from his patrols, but the evidence couldn't be ignored. Someone had invaded his territory and was killing his men. From the number of patrols that had been hit, it was a force of some size. It was bad enough that his troops were being killed, but the biggest problem was that he had no idea who was responsible for this operation.

He knew that it was definitely not the Thai military moving against him this time. His contact in the Thai defense ministry had assured him of that, and Lim had no reason to doubt him. The man had been on Kuhn Sa's payroll for far too long for him to try to lie about something like that. That left the meddling Americans, which squared with other information he had received.

He had learned that the Bangkok DEA station chief had been staying in Nakhon Phanom for the past couple of days. It was obvious that the Americans were up to something, and it was possible that the jungle invaders were DEA men, too. He made inquiries to his Bangkok DEA contacts, as well, but they were always slow to respond.

He had everyone in Kuhn Sa's far-flung network looking for answers. But until he got them, there was little he could do to counter what was happening. Beyond putting all of the troop units on full alert and sending more men out into the jungle, he could only wait for more information.

If he learned that the DEA was behind the operation in the jungle, Kuhn Sa would get hold of his contacts in the Thai government and create an international incident that would force the Americans to recall their operation. That was the best thing about the DEA—the agency was always subject to the whims of politics and politicians, particularly the senator Kuhn Sa had in his pocket.

Even if he could get this ground incursion shut down, he would still have the problem of the Yankee pilot and the stolen helicopter. According to his Nakhon Phanom agents, the Huey was being hidden from sight in the same hangar that the Harrier had used and it was also being guarded. There was no way that he could launch a successful attack on it even if he'd had another assault team to use.

Obviously, since he had a report about Grimaldi getting armament for the chopper, the pilot was outfitting it for a retaliatory raid. Nothing else made sense at all. The question was, why was he planning to use that particular helicopter instead of an American military jet fighter like the one he had used before?

The answer to that question came to him suddenly. Grimaldi was planning to use the stolen chopper because it was one of Kuhn Sa's ships. Anyone seeing it on the way in would think that it was friendly and wouldn't fire on it. They also wouldn't report seeing it, and that had to be a key part of his plan.

That problem could easily be taken care of, however. He would order a special marking painted on the belly of all the machines in the helicopter fleet and inform the troops that any ship not bearing the marking was an enemy. It would have to be something easily recognizable from the ground, maybe a large white circle.

That would also keep the missile gunners from shooting down the wrong helicopter. The Stinger missiles Kuhn Sa had flown in would also make a difference. Lim was aware of how much trouble they had caused the Red air force in Afghanistan. They would cause Grimaldi the same trouble if he attempted to attack the camp.

IN THE DAYS since Grimaldi had escaped in the Huey, Bolan had prowled the jungles like a hunting tiger. And like a tiger, he had drawn blood. In those few short days, he had chalked up a sizable body count in ambushes and attacks on unsuspecting campsites and roving patrols.

Now the patrols that were being sent out were larger. He was no longer running into two- and three-man patrols like he had seen a few days ago. When the troops were venturing out of their camps, they were going in at least squad strength and were more heavily armed.

Bolan also found that the opposition was keeping better guard on their patrol camps at night. But that hadn't been a problem for him. Attacking the camps was a losing proposition that he wanted no part of.

However, that hadn't kept him from lobbing a stick grenade past a sentry's head to explode in the squad's midst before fading into the dark.

As well as his one-man campaign was going, Bolan knew that it was time for him to end phase one of the operation and go on to phase two, the destruction of the Freehand jump jet. And as he knew only too well, phase two wasn't going to be easy.

The good thing was that his preying on Kuhn Sa's troops had to have pulled more and more of them away from the jet's base camp. From the number of patrols he had seen, most of Kuhn Sa's strength was beating the bushes looking for him instead of guarding the base camp. That had been a prime motive for his declaring a one-man war on the drug lord's troops. Fewer troops at the base camp meant that he would have fewer to deal with when he finally made his move against the jet.

The only thing that kept him from striking at the renegade jump jet was Grimaldi. The pilot had promised that he would come back, and Bolan believed him. The only thing that would prevent his return would be death or imprisonment. Nonetheless, he could wait only another day or two at the most for him to show up. If he hadn't returned by then, the warrior would have to act alone.

If he had to attempt to destroy the Yak himself, he would need a weapon powerful enough to take it out without his having to get within arm's reach of it. As he had learned from his abortive night raid, the fighter was too well guarded for him to get close. An RPG-7 antitank rocket launcher, however, could reach it from eight hundred yards out. As soon as he could capture one, he would be ready.

WHILE GRIMALDI WAS READY, the Huey wasn't. A last-minute problem had shown up in the rebuilt hydraulic system, and the mechanics were trying to repair it. While the Marines were working on the bird, he came up with one of his brighter ideas.

As long as he was basing himself out of Nakhon Phanom, he was within reach of Kuhn Sa's people. But if there was some way he could move the chopper into the jungle, hiding it like the Yak, no one would be able to get to him. The only thing that kept him from doing this was his need to refuel, but he thought of a way to get around the problem.

Remembering the extra fuel bladders that C-130s carried in their cargo bays for long-range trips, he decided he would try that method. He couldn't count on finding a fuel bladder the right size to fit in the Huey, but there was nothing to keep him from filling fifty-five-gallon steel drums with JP-4 fuel and strapping them down in the troop compartment. By adding a portable manual fuel pump, he could refuel the ship himself and extend his time in the jungle to at least two days, maybe three.

Along with the armament package and the ammunition, the fuel drums would put him beyond the maximum recommended takeoff weight for a C-model Huey. But he had flown overloaded before and knew the ship could take it, as long as he did his on-the-ground refueling in the flats with their lower air density, not in the thin air on top of a mountain.

Captain Jenson shook his head when Grimaldi brought his idea to him. "Man, you're crazed with the heat. That thing's a helicopter, not a flying dump truck."

When the pilot explained it, though, the maintenance officer had to agree that the plan might work. "I guess it'll work. I'm just glad I'm not going along as your copilot."

To save having to wrestle heavy filled drums into the chopper, six empty fifty-five-gallon fuel drums were laid on their sides in the Huey's troop compartment and securely fastened to the floor plates with steel cables and turnbuckles. Then the fuel truck was driven into the hangar and the drums were filled in place.

18

When Grimaldi stepped out of the pilot's ready room early the next morning, he was rigged for war. He wore a GI-issue 9 mm Beretta riding in a shoulder holster and another 9 mm pistol strapped to his waist in a field-belt holster. A Ka-bar fighting knife was tied to his right boot top, and he had an M-16 slung over his right shoulder. In his hands the pilot carried a 40 mm M-79 Thumper grenade launcher.

Ammunition for this arsenal was hung all over his body. The M-16 magazines were in the pouches on the front of his belt. OD cloth bandoliers of 40 mm grenades were slung over his left shoulder, and several pistol-magazine pouches were fixed to his shoulder-holster rig.

"You think you've got enough guns?" Ransom ventured to ask. The DEA station chief had come back to see the pilot off. No matter how this turned out, he had provided as much help as he could. He'd committed himself and would stand by that commitment.

Grimaldi grinned. "Since I couldn't find a way to carry an M-60 in the cockpit with me, this'll have to do. If they shoot my ass down again and I survive the crash, I want to be able to protect myself, you know what I mean?''

Ransom stuck out his hand. "I hope you get there in time to get your friend back."

Grimaldi grinned as he took his hand. "Thanks. And I want to thank you for your help. I couldn't have done this without you."

"I'll be standing by here until you get back, and I'll have the doctor on call in case you guys need him."

"Good idea."

Grimaldi was in a hurry to get in the air, but he still took the time to make a thorough walk-around inspection of the Huey. As fast as the Marines had been working on the machine, it would have been easy for them to miss something that could cause him trouble later. Of all the missions he had ever flown, this wasn't the one to relax on.

When everything from the "Jesus nut" on the top of the rotor masthead to the feed belts for the fifties had been checked out, Grimaldi opened the left-hand door to check the packages in the copilot's seat. Two rucksacks packed with food, water, AK-47 magazines and grenades had been loaded in and tied down with quick releases. Both of them also contained radio batteries, a compass and maps in plastic bags. In case he couldn't land, he would drop them both to Bolan in hopes that he could recover at least one of them.

He walked around to the right side of the ship, climbed in and strapped himself into the pilot's seat. Looking over both shoulders to make sure that the mechanics were clear of the rotors, he signaled them to open the hangar doors. His hands flew through the start-checklist procedures, and when his finger pressed the start trigger on the collective control stick, the turbine ignited.

The old familiar smell of burning kerosene quickly filled the hangar, and the roar of the turbine sounded loud even through his earphones. As soon as the EGT gauge indicated that the turbine was up to operating temperature, Grimaldi was ready to go and motioned for everyone to stand clear.

Pulling just enough pitch on the main rotor to take the weight off the skids, he carefully fed in a little cyclic, and the chopper slowly started forward with the skids scraping the concrete. It was risky to start a take-off inside the hangar, but he didn't want any extra exposure while the Marines towed the machine outside. If Kuhn Sa's people were watching, they would have to spot him quickly or he'd be long gone.

When Captain Jenson signaled that the tail boom and rotor had cleared the door, he fed in more pitch and cyclic. Going into a low ground-effect hover, he aimed the nose of the ship at the runway and taxied out to the takeoff position at the end of the main runway.

Loaded down with the guns, ammunition and extra fuel the way he was, Grimaldi decided to make a gunship takeoff to save the aging metal in the turbine and transmission the strain of a vertical takeoff. Once he was lined up on the main runway, he twisted the throttle all the way to 110 percent rpm and pushed forward on the cyclic control. The tail came up like an angry scorpion, and the Huey started down the runway.

When the airspeed built to a hundred miles per hour, he eased back on the cyclic, and the heavily laden Huey slowly lifted into the air. Five hundred feet above ground, he stomped down on the rudder pedal, racked the machine up on her right side and pointed the nose to the northeast.

He had promised Bolan that he would be back, and Jack Grimaldi always kept his promises.

EVEN THOUGH GRIMALDI'S chopper had been in sight for the absolute minimum amount of time needed to take off, once more Major Lim's network of spies and agents in Nakhon Phanom were on duty. They saw his takeoff, and right after the Huey banked away to the northeast, they made their report. Within minutes the warning message was being radioed to Lim's headquarters in the jungle.

For all of the precautions he had taken, Grimaldi wouldn't reach the Golden Triangle unannounced.

MAJOR LIM PUT DOWN the radio handset and called for his duty runner. "Tell the Russian that the American is coming."

"At once, Major."

As he had done while waiting for the Harrier to make its move, Yuri Galan had been spending his days in his flight suit. When the runner gave him the message, all he had to do was grab his helmet and gloves and head for the door at a dead run.

Galan's crew chief was seated in the cockpit again, spooling up the turbines, when the pilot dashed into the clearing. When he spotted the Russian, he scrambled out to make room for him.

As soon as Galan was buckled in and his suit connections had been secured, he advanced the throttle for his main engine and the Yak rolled out into the clearing. A quick look around as he vectored the rear nozzle to the full-down position showed him that he was clear. The Russian hit the throttles for the lift jets and the main turbine. Dust and debris swirled around him as the camouflaged Yak-141B rose in the air on the lift jets. As soon as he had fifty meters clearance above the tops of the trees, he rotated the rear jet nozzle to horizontal and opened the throttle.

As the Yak transitioned to level flight, Galan closed the lift jet's intake and cleaned up the airframe for high-speed flight. He opened the throttle all the way to the full afterburner position, and the Yak shot forward, breaking Mach unity. Then he pulled the fighter into a steep climb over the jungle.

If he ever missed the convenience of having a ground-control radar station to provide him with a vector to the bogie, this was the time. Without intercept guidance from radar, all he could do was get enough altitude, head in the direction that Grimaldi should be coming from and use his own targeting radar to try to spot him.

WHEN GRIMALDI REACHED the edge of his search area, he climbed several thousand feet higher over the jungle before he tried to contact Bolan. Radio waves work in line of sight, so he had to be well above the many hills in the area for Bolan to receive his signal. If, of course, the warrior's small survival radio was still working. The battery should have lasted this long if the radio had been switched over to the receive-only mode. The Executioner was an old hand at this game and would have done that almost automatically.

Grimaldi switched the Huey's UHF radio over to the search-and-rescue frequency and keyed the mike. "Striker," he called, "this is Flyboy. Over."

There was no answer.

"Striker, this is Flyboy. I say again, this is Flyboy. Do you copy? Over?"

He didn't immediately worry when there was no answer. He was still on the edge of the area, and there was no telling where Bolan was now. He continued flying deeper into the jungle for another fifteen minutes before trying again.

"Striker, Striker," Grimaldi radioed. "This is Flyboy on SAR push. Over.

"Come on, Mack," the pilot muttered under his breath, "answer the damned radio."

"Flyboy," came the familiar voice over Grimaldi's headphones, "this is Striker. Over."

"This is Flyboy. Activate your locator transmitter. Over."

"Striker, roger. Sending now."

The search-and-rescue locator display on the instrument panel started beeping and showed a blinking red dot. The needle of the SAR direction finder showed that he was somewhere to the northeast.

"This is Flyboy. I have your location and am about twenty mikes out. Try to find me a landing zone. Over."

"This is Striker. That's a negative on an LZ in this area. The place is crawling with the opposition, and it's not safe to set down. Over."

"Can you stop long enough to take a quick drop?" Grimaldi replied. "I've got a resupply drop ready for you—food, water and ammunition. There's also some maps and batteries for your radio. Over."

"That's most affirm. Call me again when you get in the area. I should be able to get a visual and vector you into a DZ for a fast drop."

"Roger, I'm on the way. Anything further?"

"Be advised that you are expected," Bolan transmitted. "The opposition has brought in Stingers to defend the target."

That changed the equation. Shoulder-fired, heat-seeking Stinger antiaircraft missiles were a little more than Grimaldi wanted to deal with. He didn't want his name added to the long list of those who had fallen to that marvel of American technology.

The rattletrap Huey wasn't equipped with either missile-launch detectors or decoy flare launchers to draw away a heat-seeking missile. If someone popped off a Stinger, it would fly right up his tail pipe and he'd be dog meat scattered all over the jungle.

Stingers or not, screw it, he was going in. He'd flown worse ships under worse circumstances and all they could do was kill him. But before they did, they would sure as hell know that he'd been there.

"Good copy on the Stingers. I'll worry about them later. Out."

Almost a half hour later, Grimaldi got on the radio again. "Striker, this is Flyboy. Over."

"Striker, go."

"You should be able to hear me now. Over."

"Roger," Bolan answered. "I've got you at my ten o'clock, heading northeast. Your DZ is a small clearing to your three o'clock. The wind is out of the east, and I'll be in the wood line on the south side. Over."

"Roger," Grimaldi answered. "I've got your Delta Zulu in sight. I'm coming in from the west and will go into a high hover to kick the package out."

"Roger, I'll be waiting. Out."

Grimaldi lined up on the small clearing and dropped the collective to kill some of his lift. Holding the cyclic with his knees, he reached over to unlatch the copilot's door. When he reached the DZ, all he needed to do was hit the quick release and push the rucksack out the door. He'd be vulnerable for a few seconds at most.

THE SERGEANT LEADING the patrol heard the sound of the helicopter's rotors as Grimaldi made the approach to the supply drop. He hadn't been informed of any helicopter operations in his patrol area and needed to check this out. He knew that there was a small clearing a few hundred meters ahead and signaled for his squad to double-time.

When he got close enough to spot the approaching helicopter through the brush, the sergeant saw that it looked like one of Kuhn Sa's own ships. It was painted the mat dark green of the drug lord's choppers. But, it didn't have a big white circle painted on its belly. He suddenly remembered the stolen helicopter Major Lim had radioed him to be on the lookout for, the one the American had taken. This had to be it.

He signaled for his squad to spread out and called the RPG gunner to his side. The soldier loaded a rocket-propelled grenade into the front of the launcher, flipped the sights up and cocked the firing hammer. At this range, it would be impossible for him to miss.

"Fire!" the sergeant commanded.

The gunner squeezed the trigger, and the 85 mm rocket leaped from the launcher with a whoosh.

19

Bolan stood back in the wood line at the edge of the clearing, watching Grimaldi make his approach. Suddenly, from the other side of the clearing, he heard the distinctive sound of an RPG rocket-prop charge igniting. The boom and hiss of a round leaving the launch tube was a sound a man never forgot.

"Jack!" he yelled out over the radio. "Pull pitch!"

Grimaldi reacted instantly. Reactions sharply honed in a dozen war zones had taught him never to question shouted warnings. In a situation like this, he who questioned was usually lost.

Twisting the throttle hard against the stop, he hauled up sharply on the collective. With the turbine screaming and the main rotor blades clawing the air, the Huey leaped back into the air.

The RPG rocket passed under the belly of the chopper, missing him by mere inches.

Stomping down on the right pedal, Grimaldi let the massive torque of the main rotor spin the Huey around to face his enemies. The RPG was a dangerous opponent, but he knew that the launcher took several seconds to reload and resight. So rather than try to run from it, he decided to turn on his attackers.

They were close enough that he didn't even pull his swing-away gunsight in front of his face before he fired. His M-1A1-trained eyeballs would be sight enough. Stepping on the floor-mounted trigger to his gun package, he fired the .50-caliber machine guns.

Using the chopper's controls, he marched the red tracers directly into his primary target, the two men with the RPG launcher. Once the big guns had the range, he unleashed two of the 2.75-inch rockets.

The rockets left the pods with a whoosh, trailing dirty white smoke the short distance to the target. The rockets were tipped with antipersonnel warheads that exploded into hundreds of nail-size, red-hot fragments upon impact. The detonations of the warheads sent puffs of flame-shot, dirt-black smoke erupting in the vegetation. The singeing shrapnel scythed through both the underbrush and the men hiding in it.

The rocket gunner and his sergeant collected most of the shrapnel from the rocket that exploded in front of them. Grimaldi saw them disappear behind the smoke. The other rocket took out more of the squad. The survivors tried to flee into the jungle, but Grimaldi had their range and the machine guns spoke again.

The inch-and-a-half long, heavy machine gun rounds easily cut through the brush and found their soft targets. The damage a .50-caliber round could do to the human body had to be seen to be believed. Chunks of bloody flesh were torn off, heads were exploded. There was no escape when Ma Deuce spoke.

While Grimaldi unleashed the fury of a gunship attack, Bolan raced around the perimeter of the small clearing to lend the weight of his firepower to the fight. Grimaldi had the drop on them, but the warrior knew how easy it was to shoot down a hovering chopper. A single AK round in the wrong place and he'd be history.

When the Executioner got close enough to bring his AK into play, he saw that the machine guns and rockets had done most of the work for him. All that was left was to make sure that the few seriously wounded received mercy rounds.

Now that Bolan was on them and was masking his fire, Grimaldi sent the Huey into a wide orbit over the clearing in case his friend needed more aerial fire support. When the Executioner stepped back out into the open, Grimaldi keyed his mike. "What does it like look down there?"

"We're clear here. But you'd better make the drop and get the hell out. If there's anyone else in the vicinity, they'll come running. I'll get in contact with you later."

"Roger, here it comes."

Grimaldi broke out of his orbit and made a low, fast pass over the clearing. As he approached Bolan, he reached over, tripped the release on one of the rucksacks and pushed it out the door. The package tumbled free and fell to earth.

"I've got the ruck," Bolan radioed back. "Now get out of here before someone shows up and pops another rocket at you!"

"Roger that," the pilot answered as he fed pitch to the main rotor. "I'm climbing out now. Stay on the radio and we'll set up another LZ."

"Let me get out of the area first. Then I'll change the battery and get back to you in an hour."

"Roger, out."

As the radio went dead, Grimaldi wondered if that was the last time he would see his old friend alive. It was obvious that Major Lim was gunning for them and he had the numbers on his side.

YURI GALAN HELD his Yak VSTOL fighter in a wide, loitering orbit at only fifteen thousand feet. If Grimaldi was coming, he would be coming in low, not high. But with his "look down-shoot down" radar, he should still be able to pick up the American with no problem. And when he did, that same radar would direct a missile or cannon shells to a sure strike on the target. As soon as he spotted the helicopter, Jack Grimaldi would die.

He almost wished that Grimaldi was flying another Harrier so this could be more than just an aerial ambush. There would be no classic dogfight between aerial warriors this time. It would be just a lock-on-and-fire situation. But that's all the situation really called for. As far as he was concerned, Grimaldi had violated the chivalry of the air by trying to destroy his Yak on the ground. Because of that, he deserved no better than to be destroyed without warning the instant he was spotted.

Plus, Galan had already defeated him in the air once, and were he to do it again, it would be no great feat. The American was obviously not in his league. When he went up against another pilot, he wanted it to be someone he hadn't tried before, a new conquest, as it were.

Shooting him down was just taking care of unfinished business, and the sooner it was done, the better.

IT HAD BEEN ALMOST an hour since Galan had taken off, and he finally had a radar sighting that looked promising. The radar was giving him a stationary target, though, not the slow-moving one the Russian pilot had expected. But Grimaldi was flying a helicopter, and the American might have gone into a hover for some reason.

Whatever it was, Galan wasn't going to pass it up. If the contact turned out to be nothing, he would climb back to altitude and continue his search. His gloved fingers reached out to flick on his arming panel, and he selected his 30 mm belly cannons.

He retarded his throttle and cracked his dive brakes as he nosed the Yak over into a dive. To check out the sighting, he didn't need to be flying at supersonic speeds. His radar was still showing the target, but he couldn't pick out anything against the mottled greens of the jungle.

Suddenly he spotted two puffs of white smoke trailing into the jungle. The helicopter had just fired rockets at a target on the ground. That had to be Grimaldi.

When he looked closer, he could barely make out the spinning disk of the chopper's main rotor. The dark, mat green camouflage paint of the fuselage was all but invisible against the verdant jungle. As he got closer, though, he was able to make out the tail boom and its spinning tail rotor. It was him all right.

As the Yak fell from the sky, Galan saw the chopper break out of its hover and go into an orbit over a clearing. Then it broke out of the orbit and flew away to the north. It was a perfect setup. He was coming in from the south and wouldn't even have to change his dive path to make the run. Grimaldi wouldn't even see him before he died.

A GLINT OF LIGHT off of a polished canopy high above him caught Grimaldi's eye, and he looked up. Silhouetted against a china blue sky was the distinctive shape of Galan's twin-tailed Yak-141B. The jet had the jump on him and was dropping for the kill.

Holding the cyclic stick with his knees, the Stony Man pilot reached out with his left hand and switched on his makeshift armament system, then selected the fifties. He didn't have an air-to-air gunsight, but he pulled out the fold-away ground-attack sight and flicked it on. He had already recalibrated it for the fifty's trajectory, and the guns had been bore-sighted to converge their fire at five hundred yards.

He had a thousand .50-caliber rounds per gun in each feed belt, and that had to be more ammunition than the Freehand was carrying for the 30 mm cannons in her belly. Modern fighters depended more on gun-laying radar to make their hits than they did their ammunition load. It was true that the 30 mms were formidable weapons. It would take very few of their HE shell strikes to tear the Huey apart in midair. But, pound for pound, he had more firepower on board, and the punch of the fifties was not to be discounted. All he had to do was put it on the target before the target put it on him.

His biggest problem was that the Huey was heavily loaded. It was true that he had burned off some of the fuel in the internal tanks, but he still had the full fifty-five-gallon drums strapped down in the troop compartment. That was going to make him slower than he would have liked, but it was too late now to unstrap them and kick them out. He just hoped that they had been tied down well enough to withstand the maneuvering. If one of them broke loose, it would be all over.

One thing in his favor was that he had both of the side doors closed. That would cut his drag and allow him to make better use of what speed he could coax from the turbine. Cracking the throttle past the stop to 110 percent, he got ready to make his opening move.

If he wasn't careful, he'd trash the turbine at that rpm level and crash. But if he didn't have as much airspeed as possible, he'd die. It wasn't really much of a choice.

ON THE GROUND, Bolan saw the Yak before he heard the scream of its turbine. A fast-moving speck in the sky caught his eye. "Jack," he radioed, "you've got a bogie coming down on your six."

"Roger, I'm on him," was Grimaldi's curt reply.

Bolan refrained from saying anything else to the pilot. Grimaldi didn't need the distraction of a radio message right now. Once again, the warrior had to take a back seat while his friend fought for his life in the air. And, as before, there was nothing he could do to influence the outcome of this aerial combat.

Now he wished that he had gone ahead and tried for the Yak alone. On the ground, he wouldn't have hazarded Grimaldi's life. But the die had been cast and the play would have to run to its conclusion.

GRIMALDI DIDN'T WANT to telegraph his move, but by turning the nose of his ship slightly to the right, he was able to look up over his shoulder and watch the Yak come down on him. The Russian fighter was making a standard high speed jet approach, which was in his favor. Even though the jump jet could hover like a helicopter, it couldn't slow down once it was committed to a dive like that.

Rather than cut it too fine in case Galan had a hot trigger finger, Grimaldi kicked down on the right rudder pedal and slammed the cyclic over hard right, snapping the Huey's nose around to face the jet. He pulled back on the cyclic and went into a zoom climb directly at it.

The Yak was nose on to him now, and the Huey's turbine exhaust was facing away. With the rotor blast dispersing the hot gasses, it would be difficult for the jet's heat-seeking missiles to get a lock on. That still left the Russian his 30 mm belly cannons, but they were easier to face than a guided missile.

GALAN WAS CONCENTRATING on the lighted pip in his radar gun sight, waiting for it to blink red to give him a lock on. The fact that the Huey had turned to face him didn't register in his mind until it was almost too late.

Twin streaks of red tracer fire rushed up from the chopper directly at him.

Suddenly this wasn't the simple aerial execution he had thought it would be. He was in a real dogfight with the helicopter.

20

In the split second before Grimaldi's tracers could reach up to him, Galan hit the canard and thrust-vectoring controls, snapping up the nose of his fighter as hard as he could. As the .50-caliber tracers flashed past his canopy, he banked up on one wing, dropped his nose again and triggered his 30 mm belly cannons.

He had Grimaldi in his pipper diamond, and it looked like his tracers would be on target. But the chopper spun and was no longer in the line of fire.

As maneuverable as his VSTOL fighter was, a helicopter was even more so—particularly when it was operating in a low-speed tactical envelope and didn't have to bleed off airspeed to make a sharp turn.

As Galan pulled out of his dive and racked the fighter up on one side to turn into Grimaldi, his hand reached out to activate the underwing Atoll missiles. The American pilot might be able to outmaneuver his cannon fire, but there was no way that he could run away from a heat-seeking missile. Had the Russian been thinking properly, he would have used them in the first place.

Before the missile-guidance heads could spin up, purge and lock on, the chopper spun under its rotor disk and fired again. Galan saw the winking of the muzzle blasts of the two machine guns and snap-rolled to the right to break off the attack. But the chopper nimbly turned with him and continued firing.

The Russian felt his airframe take hits and instinctively hunched behind his seat armor. Sweeping his eyes over the instrument panel, he saw no sign of fire. There were no warning lights blinking, but that didn't mean that he hadn't sustained some damage, and he knew the dangers of trying to fight with a damaged machine.

Grabbing the throttle, he shoved it past the stop into the full afterburner position. It was time to get out of the area while he still could.

The Yak surged under him as it went supersonic in a slight climb. He was out of range of Grimaldi's punishing guns in a flash.

THE ROAR of the Yak's turbine on full afterburner echoed over the jungle as Galan fled north. He was going so fast that Grimaldi didn't even try to send a few more rounds after him. From the way the Russian had broken off the combat, he had to have hit something with one of his bursts.

Grimaldi had no problem with that. The Russian had had all the advantages and he was lucky to have gotten out of it alive. The results did prove, though, the old adage that said overconfidence is the biggest killer on the battlefield. Galan had figured him for an easy kill and had been rudely awakened to the facts. The

Stony Man pilot knew that if he had to face the Yak again, however, it wouldn't turn out the same way.

"Are you okay?" Bolan radioed.

"Roger." The pilot looked around the inside of his ship as he backed his throttle down to cruising speed. "I've got a couple of holes in the sheet metal, but nothing vital seems to be damaged. I do have to find a place where I can set down while I check this bird over and make sure she's okay."

"Make it somewhere within a two hour march or so, and I'll join up with you there."

"Roger," Grimaldi answered. "Keep your map handy, and I'll give you a call when I find a spot."

"Roger that."

Keeping low to the trees, Grimaldi flew west, leaving Bolan to follow him on the ground.

WHEN GALAN REPORTED to Major Lim after landing, the Chinese officer was enraged. "You let him get away!" he shouted in disbelief. "Where did he go?"

"I do not know," the Russian replied with a shrug. "My radar showed him flying to the south."

"Why did you let him get away?"

"My aircraft had taken hits, and it has to be completely inspected before I can engage him again."

"You were not supposed to let something like this happen. You were hired because you were supposed to be a skilled pilot, not a novice."

"If you think you can fly that fighter better than I can, Major, feel free to do so. Until then, I have had about enough of your ranting and raving. I hired on to fly that plane for Kuhn Sa, not to listen to you yell at me."

Lim came out of his chair, his hand clawing at the Makarov holstered on his belt. "You cannot talk to me that way, you unwashed barbarian!"

"I can as long as Grimaldi has that helicopter out there," Galan pointed out as he stiffened to a position of attention. "I have done my job, Major. You should do yours as well as I have. Remember, I am not the one who allowed the American to escape from my custody."

Lim had the pistol out of his holster when a sudden bark in Chinese caused him to turn and slowly lower the Makarov. Kuhn Sa stood in the doorway. His bodyguards had their AKs leveled on the two men.

"I understand that you were surprised in the air today, Captain Galan," Kuhn Sa said in accented English.

"Yes, sir. I was not expecting the American to try to get into a dogfight with me in a helicopter."

"Mr. Grimaldi has proved to be a man of many talents. It would be wise not to underestimate him again."

"I will be ready for him the next time, sir," Galan vowed.

"And when will that be? I understand that your fighter was hit in your fight."

"I could not find any major damage, but my crew chief is making a complete inspection of the machine right now. I should have the report within the hour."

"Tell me exactly what happened," the drug lord ordered.

Galan quickly recounted his scramble when the alert was sent, his hour-long search for Grimaldi and his abortive attack.

"You say that he was on a hover over a clearing when you first saw him?" Kuhn Sa asked.

"Yes, sir."

"What was he doing there?"

"I do not know."

"Did you see any men in the clearing?"

Galan shook his head. "No, sir. I was concentrating on shooting him down and did not look at anything else."

"Show me where this happened."

When Galan pointed the area out on the big map on Lim's wall, Kuhn Sa said something in Chinese to Lim, who nodded and, after checking a roster, answered.

"One of the major's patrols is in that area, and it will be sent to investigate this clearing. If he was hovering there, he might have been contacting a ground unit."

The drug lord turned back to the pilot. "You will see to your airplane and be ready to shoot Mr. Grimaldi down as soon as he shows up."

"Yes, sir."

As Galan walked away, he could hear Kuhn Sa berating Lim in loud, rapid-fire Chinese. He was glad that he was still on the drug lord's good side. But he knew that one more screwup and he'd be finished.

THREE HOURS AFTER GRIMALDI flew off, Bolan reached the area where the pilot had radioed that he was setting down. He checked the jungle around the LZ for a quarter mile to make sure that it was clear before he moved in to join him. Even though he had the exact coordinates, the Huey was so well hidden that he almost missed it.

Grimaldi had set the chopper down through a break in the jungle canopy that was barely large enough to clear the spinning rotor disk. In fact, the tips of the blades had trimmed a few of the branches on the way down. For him to get out of there, he would have to keep the chopper exactly vertical for the first forty feet to clear the trees. But if Grimaldi had been able to get the Huey in there, he would be able to get it back out.

Not content to rely on the mat green paint to hide the chopper from aerial observation, Grimaldi had cut jungle foliage and draped it over the machine. Branches and fronds were hanging from the two-bladed main rotor, and other foliage was stacked on the canopy to hide any possible reflection. The tail boom had been completely hidden with vines and broad leaves. It would take a sharp eye in a low-flying chopper to spot it.

Since the pilot had an M-16 slung over his shoulder, Bolan called out before stepping into the open.

Grimaldi grinned when he saw his friend. "I told you I'd come back."

"I never doubted it."

Bolan looked at the rocket pods and .50-caliber guns mounted on the Huey. "And you came with help. Where'd you get all the hardware?"

"Our friend Ransom has a friend in the Thai air force who's got his hand out. He lends things like gunship packages to the DEA for the right price."

"That sounds familiar."

Bolan's eyes ran the length of the chopper. "Speaking of guns, did you take any hits?"

"Nothing serious. There are some new holes in the sheet metal," Grimaldi replied, nodding toward the three 30 mm cannon holes in the side doors. "Including one in the tail boom. But that seems to be it, and it's nothing that will keep me from finishing the job."

"What do you need to do to get ready?"

"The first thing I want to do is refuel so I can get those drums out of the back and lighten the ship. There's no way that I can lift out of here with them still on board."

Bolan dropped his rucksack in the copilot's seat, but left his AK slung over his shoulder. "Let's do it."

The two men manhandled the fifty-five-gallon drums of fuel into place in the open door so the manual pump could be hooked up to them. Once that was done, all it took was for one man to pull the pump handle back and forth to transfer the fuel while the other one held the end of the pump hose in the fuel filler neck. It was slow work even with the two men spelling each other on the pump.

As soon as the Huey was completely topped off, they rolled the empty drums back into the jungle so they couldn't be spotted from the air after the chopper was gone. The key to the success of the operation was to keep the opposition guessing, and a big part of that was preventing them from discovering where they had spent the night.

Once everything had been taken care of, the two men broke out rations from Bolan's pack. Now that the sun was down, there was nothing for either of them to do but wait out the night. After a quick meal of MRE rations borrowed from the Marines, they made themselves comfortable in the troop compartment of the chopper.

"You're one loss, one tie and no wins against that guy, so what do you want to do next?" Bolan asked.

Grimaldi shook his head. "The smart thing would be for both of us to get in the bird, go back to Nakhon Phanom and let someone else deal with that Freehand."

"That would probably be the smart thing," Bolan agreed. "But since neither one of us is well-known for doing the smart thing on something like this, do you have any suggestions?"

Grimaldi shrugged. "I guess I'll just go up again tomorrow and try my luck with Galan again."

"Rather than depending on luck," the warrior replied, "why don't we stack the deck in our favor?"

"What do you have in mind?"

"What do you think about us pulling an Air Cavstyle miniair assault?"

The Stony Man pilot squinted in momentary confusion. "You mean like we did back in our soldiering days?"

"Why not? You're a one-man Red Team, and I can play the role of the Blues."

"Geez, man, are you sure you haven't been in the jungle too long?"

"It worked way back when."

"Yeah, but we both probably had the numbers on our side. We don't have a company backing us up this time."

Bolan grinned. "I thought you and I were supposed to be worth at least a battalion."

"That, too, was back in the good old days. We're probably only worth a squad now. So what's the plan?"

Bolan took out the map from his rucksack and spread it on the ground. Snapping on Grimaldi's red-lensed flashlight, he focused the beam on the unmarked spot where the Yak's base camp was located.

"The way I see it, we've got to get that plane while it's on the ground. You've gone up against it twice now and haven't done all that well."

Grimaldi couldn't argue with that logic. The simple fact was that Galan was a hell of a pilot and he was flying an even better airplane. "Exactly how do you want to work this air-assault scheme of yours?"

"Just like in the good old days of Nam. I'll go in after the target while you fly air cover and keep them busy. But since I've seen some of the patrols carrying Stingers, you're only going to be able to make one high-speed pass."

His finger traced a flight path on the map. "Come in low from the northeast, dump all the ordnance you've got, then get out of the area."

"And what will you be doing?"

"Like I said, I'll be in position, so I take the Yak out with that M-79 I saw in the cockpit."

Grimaldi smiled in the dark. "It sounds a lot like the good old days."

"Doesn't it?"

21

At first light the next morning, Bolan and Grimaldi pulled the branches and foliage away from the Huey and carried them back into the wood line. If someone flew over this spot before they made the strike, they didn't want anything to look out of the ordinary.

There was little said as the two men readied the chopper for takeoff. They both knew what had to be done and did it. When they were strapped into their seats and the rotor was turning above them, Grimaldi keyed his intercom. "You ready for this?"

"Let's do it."

Grimaldi's deft hands on the Huey's collective and cyclic controls lifted the helicopter out of the small clearing with a minimum amount of trouble. Once above the trees, he kept low as he flew to the spot Bolan had picked the night before to begin his march into the target area.

A half hour later, Grimaldi went into a low hover over a small stream. The Executioner opened the copilot's door and stepped down onto the skid. From there it was only a short drop to the water. He raised a hand in farewell as he stepped out of the stream and set his course for the Yak's camp. He had a two-hour march ahead of him to get into position so Grimaldi could make his move.

As Bolan disappeared into the jungle, the pilot hauled up on the collective to pull pitch to the rotor and pointed the chopper to the north. Flying with the skids almost brushing the treetops, he headed for the second spot they had picked on the map.

Once he got there, he would find a concealed place to set down, shut the turbine off and wait for Bolan to get into position for the main event.

YURI GALAN BROUGHT his Yak-141B to a hover on the lift jets above the clearing at the camp. Gently retarding the throttles, he let the jump jet sink through the ring of trees. When the wheels touched down in a whirl of dust, he killed the fuel feed, and the turbine roar died.

He had been in the air for more than three hours that morning, and there had been no sign of Grimaldi and his helicopter. For all he knew, the American had flown it south and was already out of the country. Or he could have crashed somewhere and been swallowed up by the jungle. The Russian still couldn't believe that he hadn't scored enough hits in their encounter to have crippled the helicopter.

Whatever the case, he would have his machine refueled, get something to eat and get back in the air in an hour or so. Until Lim could locate Grimaldi's whereabouts, he would have to fly one-man air cover over the Golden Triangle.

As he slid the canopy back, Sergeant Chow and his men rushed out to push the fighter back into its hiding place under the camouflage net. Climbing out of his cockpit, the Russian ordered the Yak refueled before walking to Lim's headquarters to make his report.

When Galan reported to Lim, he noticed that Kuhn Sa's visit seemed to have had a strong effect on the Chinese officer. He had dropped the perpetual sneer and seemed to be honestly trying to help find the American pilot. He didn't know what Kuhn Sa had told him, but whatever it had been, he was glad not to have the man on his back.

"I sent a patrol into the area where you saw Grimaldi yesterday," Lim said after the Russian reported no contact. "And all they found were the bodies of the previous patrol. They appeared to have been killed by a gunship. Both Kuhn Sa and I think that he was trying to link up with a unit on the ground when the patrol interrupted him."

"That might be," Galan said, nodding, "but like I told the general, I was so busy trying to shoot him down that I didn't notice anyone on the ground. When I go back up, I will be on the lookout for them."

"Good," Lim replied. "The general is counting on you."

Galan was glad that Kuhn Sa had gotten Lim under control, but he was still concerned about what would happen after he had taken care of the American flier. From what he had seen, Lim was the kind of man to hold a grudge for a long time.

AFTER BOLAN REACHED the target area, it took him almost another hour to find the right position from which to launch his attack. The M-79 grenade launcher had a maximum range of four hundred meters, so he had to get in fairly close to make the hit. Even more important, he had to find a place where the trees didn't mask his line of fire. The grenades had a high trajectory and would rise above the treetops before coming back down.

Once he was settled in, he took the survival radio from his breast pocket and keyed the built-in mike. "Flyboy, Flyboy," he transmitted. "This is Striker, over."

"Flyboy, go," Grimaldi answered instantly.

"I'm in position. The Yak is on the ground where it was before. Make your run from the north, and you should be able to get a good shot at it."

"Roger," the pilot replied. "I'm cranking now. ETA your location, fifteen mikes."

"I'll be waiting. Out."

GALAN HAD FINISHED his lunch and was walking back to his fighter when he heard a faint sound and stopped. In an instant, he recognized the distinctive wop-wopping of a Huey's rotors coming fast and low.

This was the thing he had feared most. The Americans had invented the helicopter gunship and had developed their tactics into a fine art. Unfortunately he was about to experience this military art firsthand. He had underestimated Grimaldi, and now he was going to pay for that miscalculation. But if he could reach the

Yak and get it off the ground, he might be able to turn this aerial ambush around.

Major Lim also recognized the sound of the approaching helicopter and knew that the camp was under attack. Cursing the Russian pilot loudly for allowing this to happen, he ran for the door of his headquarters. One of the Stinger missile launchers was stored in the guard post right outside the building.

GRIMALDI BROUGHT the Huey in low and fast with the skids brushing the treetops and the tachometer needle bouncing well past the redline. He hoped he was flying too low and too fast for the Stinger gunners to get a lock on him. He would find out in a few seconds.

When the first of the camp's bamboo buildings came in sight, he tripped the firing trigger for the 2.75-inch rocket pods. Two rockets lanced out, trailing smoke into the trees. Before they had time to impact, he nudged the rudder pedals, lined up on another building and fired two more.

He caught a glimpse of startled troops looking up through the trees at him, and triggered the machine guns. Walking them into the target, he was rewarded with the sight of the men being blown off their feet before they had a chance to raise their AKs.

So far, so good. Now to the main event.

GALAN REACHED the Yak at a dead run. Sergeant Chow had the turbines running, but the rest of the ground crew was nowhere in sight. He cursed them for cowards as he scrambled into the cockpit.

He was still buckling his shoulder harness when he hit the throttle to roll the fighter into the open. Looking over his shoulder, he saw Grimaldi's chopper heading straight for him. He wasn't completely out from under the trees yet, but he still slammed the lift-jet controls into full throttle.

Turbines screaming, the Yak lifted her nose gear off the ground just as the tail cleared the edge of the camouflage netting. Using his vector controls, Galan slid the nose around to face away from the attacking chopper.

GRIMALDI SAW the Yak's nose come out from under the camouflage netting and sighted in on it, just as a machine gun opened up on him from a ground position. Instinctively jinking to the side to escape the ground fire threw off his aim as he hit the trigger.

The 2.75-inch rockets hit at the edge of the clearing, their blast tearing big holes in the VSTOL fighter's camouflage-netting cover.

At the speed he was traveling, Grimaldi was past the clearing in a flash and the undamaged Yak was rising on its lift jets to give chase.

SEEING THE YAK COME UP off of its landing gear as it lifted into the air, Bolan carefully sighted his grenade launcher and fired. The butt of the M-79 slammed into his shoulder as he watched the grenade arc out through the break in the trees and into the clearing.

Because the fighter was turning on its axis, the 40 mm grenade hit the fuselage a glancing blow right in front of the air intake for the main engine. It ricocheted into the intake, where it was sucked into the blades of the turbine compressor and detonated.

The explosion turned the whirling compressor blades into chunks of stainless-steel shrapnel. These many red-hot, jagged blades sliced into the Yak's fuel tanks.

Galan didn't even have time to hit his zero-altitude seat-ejector handle before the Yak's fuselage was engulfed in a ball of flame.

MAJOR LIM STOOD at the edge of the clearing with his feet spread apart as he raised the Stinger launcher to his shoulder. Kuhn Sa was going to kill him for the attack on the camp, but he wouldn't die alone. He lined up the sights on Grimaldi's retreating chopper and pressed the trigger to the first stop to purge the warhead guidance system and get a lock on.

Even over the roar of the jet's engine and the noise of the Huey's rotors, Lim recognized the characteristic thump of an American M-79 grenade launcher. He saw a grenade hit the fighter and screamed, "No!"

The Stinger launcher on his shoulder tracked naturally when the Chinese officer looked at the flaming Yak. The burning fuel provided the blind eye of the warhead guidance system a heat source to lock on to. The unknowing pressure of Lim's finger on the launcher's trigger sent the rocket on its short way.

Yuri Galan, ex-Soviet air force jet pilot turned mercenary for a drug lord, caught the flare of the Stinger's launch and screamed inside the cockpit of his fighter. The scream was cut off when the missile detonated right behind his head.

SEEING THE FIREBALL over his shoulder, Grimaldi looked in time to see the pieces of the Yak rain onto the clearing. He had missed, but the Executioner hadn't.

Stomping down on his rudder pedal, he snapped the nose of his gunship around for another pass. He remembered what Bolan had said about the Stingers, but he had to give him a chance to escape. The camp was crawling with troops, and they were racing for their perimeter positions in the jungle. A little .50-caliber fire might slow them enough for Bolan to get away.

22

As Grimaldi completed his pedal turn to point his nose back at the camp, he knew that he was pressing his luck. Nonetheless, he laid down on the machine guns' triggers as he flew low over the flaming wreckage of the Yak fighter. The big guns began to roar, the ammo feed belts vibrating as they fed the last of the cartridges into the breeches.

Stomping down alternately on the rudder pedals, he snapped the Huey's tail from side to side, spraying the deadly slugs in a wide swath in front of him. No one could stand against that storm of fire, but when he ran out of ammo, he had better be on his way out of the area as fast as he could go.

He recognized Lim at the last instant before the guns chewed him to pieces. The Chinese officer still had the Stinger launcher on his shoulder. But, from the thin smoke trailing from the end, Grimaldi knew that he had already fired the missile.

The Stony Man pilot steadied the ship to let the twin streams of fire converge and walked them over the top of the Chinese officer. He glanced down as he flashed past and saw that Lim had taken enough hits to be barely recognizable as a man. That was fine with him. He had never liked being kept in a cage.

A MILE FROM THE CAMP, Grimaldi set the Huey in a clearing, then reached over and opened the copilot's door. Crouching as he ran to clear the rotor blades, Bolan clamored in and shut the door behind him.

"Clear," he said, jerking his thumb upward as he reached behind him for his shoulder harness.

The pilot pulled pitch and the chopper rose into the air again. Grimaldi keyed the intercom as he banked away to the southwest and away from the Golden Triangle. "This is your captain speaking," he intoned. "Our next stop will be Nakhon Phanom."

Bolan settled down for the flight. Once more, payback had been delivered and there was satisfaction in that. But even with the Freehand gone, he knew that the Golden Triangle wouldn't change all that much. The heroin would still be produced as it had always been. But it wouldn't be flown to distribution points in a supersonic jet.

Also, the renegade fighter and its pilot had both been destroyed. That was supposed to make up for the lives of the men shot out of the sky, but he knew that it didn't. Nothing could make up for the great loss of life caused by the drug wars. But as he knew only too well, the wars would go on until the last opium poppy was eradicated.

The wheels of retribution are turning in Somalia

STONY MAN™ 17
VORTEX

Sanctioned to take lethal action to stop the brutal slaughter
of innocents, the Stony Man team challenges the campaign
of terror waged by two Somali warlords. But in the killing
grounds the Stony Man warriors are plunged into a full-
blown war fueled by foreign powers with a vested interest in
the outcome of this struggle.

In June, don't miss the second
fast-paced installment of

D. A. HODGMAN

STAKEOUT SQUAD
MIAMI HEAT

Miami's controversial crack police unit draws fire from all
directions—from city predators, local politicians and a
hostile media. In MIAMI HEAT, a gruesome wave of cult
murders has hit Miami, and Stakeout Squad is assigned
to guard potential victims. As panic grips the city, Stakeout
Squad is forced to go undercover…and dance with the
devil.

Don't miss MIAMI HEAT, the second installment of Gold
Eagle's newest action-packed series, STAKEOUT SQUAD!

Look for it in June, wherever Gold Eagle books are sold.